Deadly Gamble

by Connie Shelton

Intrigue Press

Copyright©1995 Connie Shelton.

Printed and bound in the United States of America. All rights reserved. No part of this book may be reproduced or transmitted in any form or by any means, electronic or mechanical, including photocopying, recording, or by an information storage and retrieval system—except by a reviewer who may quote brief passages in a review to be printed in a magazine or newspaper—without permission in writing from the publisher.

For information, please contact Intrigue Press, P.O. Box 456, Angel Fire, NM 87710. 505-377-3474

ISBN 1-890768-00-6

First printing 1995
First paperback printing 1997

This book is a work of fiction. Names, characters, places, and incidents are either products of the author's imagination or are used fictitiously. Any resemblance to actual events or locales or persons, living or dead, is entirely coincidental. Although the author and publisher have made every effort to ensure the accuracy and completeness of information contained in this book, we assume no responsibility for errors, inaccuracies, omissions, or any inconsistency herein. Any slights of people, places or organizations are unintentional.

Cover art by BJ Graphics

For Dan
The nicest guy I know.
My best friend, lover, partner and husband.
You have always believed in me.

The author wishes to acknowledge the invaluable assistance of the following people:

Dan Shelton, proofreader and technical advisor; Leslie Lenz, my editor, without whom thousands of erroneous commas would have sneaked past me; the members of the Moreno Valley Writers Guild, for their collective enthusiasm and undying support. Last, but not least, to Lady and Miss Kitty—writing would not be the same without one or both of you on my lap.

1

Working on a case for Stacy North would have probably been the last item *ever* on my agenda. Stacy had been my best friend and roommate in college. My best friend, right up until the day she eloped with my fiancè, Brad North. Although I came to realize later that it was all for the best, such situations do tend to put a damper on a friendship.

Brad went on to become a personal injury attorney, one of Albuquerque's most, shall we say, aggressive. They live in Tanoan, *the* new upscale community in town.

Now Stacy stood in my office with all the calm of a cat at the dog pound. She looked every bit of fifteen years older, a pity because it was only eight

years since the last time I'd seen her. She wore a
tailored linen dress the color of a fresh lemon, with
black trim around the neck and down the front. Gold
buttons trailed along the trim, buttons that looked
like they'd been custom made to match the earrings
that peeked demurely out of her soft blond hairstyle.
A black ranch mink contrasted strikingly with her
hair and with the dress, creating an elegant picture
of black and gold. For just a second, I wondered why
I felt sorry for her.

It was something in the eyes. And in the mouth.
Those eyes, which had sparkled with clear blue fun
in school. The mouth, always ready to laugh. Stacy
had been the practical joker, the whimsical elf
among us. All traces of that were gone now. Dull
blue eyes, rimmed by puffy lids, darted around the
room nervously. Once clear skin was now covered
with layers of makeup to conceal the woman inside.
Or perhaps to present an image, the image of a
woman someone else wanted Stacy to be.

"Charlie, I need your help." The voice was low
and cultured, and it only broke slightly on the last
word.

A rush of ambivalent feelings flooded through
me. I'd spent ten years making myself not care about
Stacy, and I wasn't sure I wanted to start again now.
She and Brad had hurt me — deeply. My first
instinct was to toss her out of my office. The despera-
tion in her eyes pulled me back, though.

"Sit down and tell me about it," I offered grudgingly. I gestured toward the room at large, giving her the choice of taking the side chair beside my desk or the sofa on the opposite wall. She chose the sofa.

She perched on the edge of the cushion making little adjustments to her skirt and coat before speaking.

"A valuable item has, ah, been lost. I have to recover it."

"I'm an accountant, Stacy. Unless it's your tax return we're talking about, I think you should be telling this to Ron. He's the investigator around here. I can have him call you when he gets back to town next week." My brother, Ron, and I are partners in RJP Investigations. Although I watch the cases that come through the door pretty closely, I prefer to stay with the accounting and let Ron do the dirty work.

"Oh, no. I can't wait until next week." Her eyes had grown wide, her breathing rapid. "I have to get this item back before tomorrow night."

"What's the item, and why the urgency?"

She squirmed in her seat a minute before answering. "My Rolex watch," she said.

"Was it lost or stolen?"

"Lost. No, I think it was stolen . . . Um, well, I'm not really sure."

"Couldn't it have been misplaced around the house somewhere?"

"No. It's not around the house somewhere." Her voice was firm, but her eyes wouldn't meet mine.

"Where did you last see it?"

"Umm . . . I'd really rather not say."

"Stacy!" I was losing patience fast. "How do expect us to find it? Give me some help here."

She stared at her hands, suddenly finding a cuticle that needed attention. I got up and closed the door softly. Pulling the side chair around to face her, I sat with my hands between my knees and waited. When she looked up, her eyes were moist.

"I first noticed it missing from the house." She gazed out the window as she spoke. "Someone must have broken in and stolen it."

"Did you report it to the police? To your insurance company?"

"No!"

"Why not?"

Her eyes touched mine for the briefest second, darted to the bookshelf, then the far wall. I waited.

"I don't want Brad to know. He already thinks I'm careless. I can't let him know I've lost the watch. It was a Valentine gift. I've only had it two weeks."

"Stacy, to put it bluntly, that's bullshit. How can Brad blame you?" I waited another long minute while she fidgeted some more.

"Well, um, it wasn't exactly a burglary," she said finally. "A man had been there that day, uh, doing some work. I think he must have picked up the watch from my dresser."

"Did you report this to the company he worked for?"

"No."

"Why not!" I felt like shaking her.

She pulled the edges of the mink together, retreating like a turtle into its shell. I reached out, laying one hand on her fur-clad knee.

"Stacy, come on. We used to be able to talk about anything." Before she and Brad eloped right under my nose. I realized I was feeling sympathetic toward her and pulled my hand back. I wasn't at all sure I wanted to rebuild a friendship with her at this point. However, her fear was evident. "I can't help you if I don't know the whole situation," I finally said.

I could almost hear her thoughts churning. After she sifted through the entire thing, I wondered what little sprinkling she'd give me. She worked again at the errant cuticle for a couple of minutes.

"The man's name is Gary Detweiller. He wasn't at the house doing work."

This time her eyes met mine firmly. I felt my mouth open, but it closed again.

"Can you help me, Charlie?"

"Brad's coming home tomorrow night, and you need to be wearing the watch, is that it?"

"Yes."

"Stacy, can I be blunt? Why would you want to tell anyone else about this? I mean, you obviously have plenty of money. Why didn't you just go out and buy another watch?"

She gave a short humorless chuckle. "For one, I don't personally have any money. I get a hundred dollars a month cash *spending money*. Over several years I've been able to stash away a little. Everything else is in joint accounts, which Brad monitors like a hawk. The clothes, the furs, the jewelry — he bestows them like rewards. Secondly, the watch was half of a matching pair. Brad bought himself one at the same time, and he made a big point of telling me how they matched exactly, down to the color of the watch face and the size of the little dots that indicate the hours. I've only worn the thing two weeks. What if I picked out a new one, and some little detail was off? He'd know in an instant."

What a mess.

"What can I do, Charlie?"

"You want to hire a private investigator to find the watch. Right?"

She nodded. I sucked on my lower lip.

"Like I said, Ron's gone until next week. Could you tell Brad you took the watch in for cleaning?"

"It's only two weeks old," she sensibly pointed out.

"Repairs?"

"Maybe, if I had to. I'm just worried that he might call the jeweler to find out what the problem is."

This poor woman really did live under the gun.

"Let me see what I can do," I said, wishing I'd

gone out of town, too. "Can you tell me anything about this Detweiler? Confidentially."

"Not much. I met him at the club. He flirted, talked me into letting him come over for a drink."

"He's a member of the country club? Does Brad know him?"

"I don't think so. I'd never seen him there before last week."

I wanted to ask whether having a drink was all they'd done, but didn't figure it was any of my business. I did ask for a five hundred dollar retainer, though. She could explain it at home any way she wanted.

Stacy left a few minutes later, the worry lines around her mouth only slightly less pronounced than when she'd walked in here. I picked up the phone book and looked up Gary Detweiler. There was only one listed. The address was in a low-to-middle income area, a place I didn't imagine produced many Tanoan Country Club members. I decided to take a drive over there.

Outside, the weather was nearly balmy — bright blue sky, temperature near sixty. Spring is an unpredictable time here. Tomorrow could very well be thirty degrees with wind, rain or sleet. In the car, I shed my jacket, debating the quickest route to Gary Detweiler's neighborhood.

Albuquerque has become a sprawling city, thirty miles in diameter, something the Spanish conquistadors probably never imagined back in the

1500s. Early city planners divided the town into quadrants — north valley, south valley, northeast heights and southeast heights, as they are commonly called today. As the population approaches the half-million mark, the outlying towns — Tijeras and Cedar Crest to the east, Bernalillo to the north, Rio Rancho on the west side, and Belen and Los Lunas toward the south — have become suburbs with thousands of daily commuters. Very few of us ride horses, wear spurs, or carry pistols on a daily basis. We do speak English and we consider New Mexico one of the fifty states, although it seems outsiders have to pause to remember this sometimes.

I left the peacefulness of our semi-residential, semi-commercial office neighborhood and joined the flow of traffic on Central Avenue. Opting to bypass downtown, I cut over to Lomas and headed east. The Sandia Mountains stood out in high relief on this clear day, like a guardian sentinel protecting the city from the ravages of the eastern plains.

Detweiller's address was in a quiet residential neighborhood between Lomas and Central that had boomed in the late fifties. Some of the places were occupied by their original owners while others had been sold and resold and converted to rentals. The condition of each house and front yard generally indicated which were which.

Detweiller's house was a stucco box placed in the middle of a gray river-rocked square of land wedged between two other similar squares of land. This one had benefit of a few shrubs. Junipers that looked like they hadn't been trimmed in a dozen years lined the empty driveway. Scraggly pyracantha flanked the front porch. Two windows faced the street, each curtained in a different color. Brown paint peeled off the front door and two newspapers lay on the step. The whole place exuded emptiness. I pressed the bell anyway and was almost glad when no one answered.

If Gary Detweiller had stolen a Rolex watch yesterday, he'd obviously used the proceeds to go elsewhere. I pictured a quick sale at a pawn shop, with the next stop Vegas.

I wasn't far off the mark. Detweiller's house was two blocks off Central Avenue, the famed old Route 66, which used to be the main drag through Albuquerque. Now it's lined with seedy motels, mobile home dealers, and plenty of pawn shops. I started with the closest one. The third stop yielded the Rolex, easily identified by the serial number Stacy had given me. I choked a little at the price I had to pay to get it back, but figured Stacy would find a way to come up with it.

When I called her scarcely two hours after our first meeting, she was astounded. We met, exchanged watch for money (she gave me an inch-high stack of tens and twenties), and that should have been the end of it.

In fact, I'm sure that would have been the end

of it, had it not been for the news item three days later announcing that Gary Detweiller had been murdered.

2

Thursday started off normally enough. I awakened about seven, fed Rusty, my rust-colored Labrador-sized mutt, and ate a bowl of granola with yogurt while Rusty crunched down a bowl of some yummy doggy nuggets. By eight o'clock, we were traveling from home in the old country club area to our office near downtown. The office, which I share with my older brother, Ron, is in an old Victorian with gray and white exterior. A driveway runs down the west edge of the property, leading to a detached garage out back and generous parking for the three of us who work there. Besides Ron and myself, we employ a part-time receptionist, Sally Bertrand.

Ron and I started the agency three years ago at

a turning point in both our lives. Ron had gone through a rough divorce, and found that his security guard salary wasn't quite making the child support payments on three kids. Bernadette had wiped out their bank account, taking the boys and everything else of value. For Ron, starting out again in a one-bedroom apartment with old cast-off furniture was a blow. He needed a purpose and a better income.

In my case, I'd finished college with an accounting degree, taken the CPA exam, and gone to work in one of the city's largest accounting firms. Two years of corporate politics, water-cooler gossip, and general backstabbing had made me more than ready for freedom. Ron and I put our skills together, along with some of my inheritance money, and started RJP Investigations. Ron's good at his work. He has connections in the police department, and the patience for surveillance work, much more necessary attributes in the PI business than a trench-coat, a smoky office, or a babe on the arm.

Sally and I keep the wheels running smoothly here. She comes in from nine to one, answering phones and typing letters. I consider Sally a friend as well as an employee, although our styles outside the office are totally different. She's an outdoor type who spends her weekends with her husband, Ross, trekking from one remote mountain top to another. Their idea of fun consists of stuffing the barest necessities of life into forty-pound backpacks and toting this burdensome load off to someplace with neither toilets nor fast food restaurants. My idea of roughing it, on the other hand, is black and white TV in a motor home.

At work we mesh well, though. Having Sally around frees up my mind for working with numbers, something I don't do well with three phone lines ringing and the front door to attend. I handle the billing, the bill paying, the taxes, and most importantly, the paychecks. Once in awhile, I get called upon to help Ron with some detail of an investigation, usually an errand to the county courthouse to look up a copy of someone's marriage license. Exciting stuff.

My Jeep was the first car in the parking area today. Sally would be here in another half-hour or so. Ron was still out of town — gone until Monday. Rusty bounded out the minute I opened the car door and proceeded to sniff the perimeter of the yard for possible overnight intruders. Since the neighborhood is still partly residential, an occasional cat wanders across our property. It's Rusty's job to assess this situation. I unlocked the back door and stepped into the kitchen. We haven't changed the layout of the old house. The original parlor is now our reception area, the dining room a conference area. Upstairs, two bedrooms facing the street became Ron's and my offices, while a third bedroom is now a storage room. The only bathroom is also up there, and has to serve both boys and girls. How *did* these Victorian families manage?

I set my briefcase on the kitchen table, leaving the door open for Rusty while I made coffee. I hoped Sally would bring doughnuts. We leave that part informal. Whoever has a craving that day will usually show up with treats. Rusty trotted in, his nails clicking on the hardwood floor. I closed the door behind him and we headed toward the front, leaving the coffee to hiss and sputter to completion. The answering machine on Sally's desk showed no messages. I unlocked the front door and proceeded upstairs with my rust-colored shadow close behind.

My office is my second home. As such, I like it comfortable. I've chosen good wood furniture, hanging ferns in the bay window, and soft pastels for the upholstery and art.

I had no sooner parked my butt in the chair than I heard the front door. We have a ding-dong type bell rigged to ring upstairs for those times when Sally isn't on duty. Like now. I pulled myself back up, trying to remember if we had any appointments on the book. I didn't think so. It's usually pretty quiet when Ron isn't here. Maybe a salesperson or a delivery. Given a choice, I would opt for the latter.

Stacy North waited in the foyer. Today she wore no makeup and her designer jogging suit looked slept in. Her feathery blond hair hung limp. Her lips looked thin without lipstick, her face grayish. I motioned her upstairs, watching her feet drag upward at each step. I offered coffee. She nodded. I trotted back down the stairs and came back with two mugs. The social formalities accomplished, I looked at her inquisitively. She handed over the morning paper tentatively before taking a seat on the sofa. The paper was folded so that page A-4 faced me. A captioned photo told me I was staring into the face of Gary Detweiller. The headline told me he'd been killed in a shooting. I read the rest of the article while Stacy perched on the edge of the couch. She was motionless except to raise the coffee mug to her lips occasionally.

Detweiller had been sitting in his car in his own driveway when an unknown assailant shot him at almost point-blank range, the article said. I pictured the heavily overgrown shrubs that bordered the drive. The victim was survived by his wife, Jean, and son, Joshua. No leads had yet been found in the case. I laid the paper on my desk and looked up at Stacy.

"This is the guy of our former discussion?"

She nodded tiredly.

"And?"

No response.

"Stacy, I assume you didn't just come by to share this with me," I said, holding the newspaper up. "What do you want?" I had a feeling I knew the answer, and I wasn't going to like it.

"I need help again, Charlie." Her voice came out thickly.

"Stacy, I told you, I'm not an investigator. Besides, aren't the police handling this?"

Her blue eyes widened slightly. "That's what I'm worried about." She reached for her bag. "Do you mind if I smoke?"

"I'd rather you didn't." It probably came out sounding harsh, but dammit, I have to live in this office after she leaves. "Stacy, you were never a smoker."

A trembling hand covered her mouth. "I know, Charlie. I only do it now and then."

"Stacy, what's really the problem here? Are you worried that the police will dig up your connection with Detweiller?"

"Of course I am!" She stood up and paced to the opposite end of the room. "Charlie, do you have any idea what Brad will do if he finds out about this?"

Truthfully, I didn't. But I also wondered aloud why she hadn't worried about this before getting seduced into the situation.

"I don't know," she said, her voice hopeless. She dumped herself back onto my couch, and rubbed at her temples with both index fingers. "It was stupid. I can see that now. I guess I just fell for the ... uh ... positive attention."

"I'm not sure what to tell you." I wanted to tell her about paying the consequences for our actions, but somehow I got the feeling she already knew about that.

She stared at a spot somewhere near the corner of my desk, and her face became even more pale. A long minute passed.

"Stacy, what do you want from me?"

"I'm not sure, Charlie. I guess I'm grasping at ways to keep my name out of this."

"Have you talked to a lawyer? Sounds like this is more a matter of needing legal advice than investigative work."

"I wouldn't know who to turn to. Our family lawyer intimidates me. He's so chummy with Brad I don't think I could trust him. I guess I was hoping that you could find out who really killed Gary before the police come asking questions of me."

The messes people get themselves into never cease to amaze me.

"Stacy, I'll tell you straight out. This is out of my league. If you can wait until Monday, I can set an appointment for you to meet with Ron."

Her eyes glistened moistly and a red rim formed around her upper lip. The hands shook as she reached for her purse. "That's four days away," she whispered. "I hope it's not too late." She walked toward the door.

"Stacy, wait." I knew this was foolish, even as I said the words.

She returned to the couch, perching expectantly on the edge.

"Tell me everything you can about Gary Detweiller," I said.

She stared blankly at me for a good half minute.

"Does he belong to the country club? What does he do for fun? Sports? Clubs? Hangouts?"

"I really don't know." Her palms fluttered upward. "I met him at Tanoan. He never talked about himself."

A man who *never* talked about himself? Please.

"Stacy, think about it. He must have said something. Surely you didn't hop into bed with someone who never said a word."

"Well, of course he talked. But mostly he talked about me." Her eyes turned dreamy. "He told me how beautiful I was, how sexy. Stuff I haven't heard in a long time." Her once-vivacious voice broke a little.

I let the silence stretch out a bit, hoping she'd come up with something more.

"I went to his house once," she remembered.

"That might be a start. Tell me about it."

"It was a depressing place. Of course, this was after he'd wooed me with a nice lunch out one day and he'd gotten a room at the Marriott that afternoon. I guess I wasn't thinking too straight."

"Then he invited you to his house?"

"Oh, no. I just showed up. I'd seen the address on a business card he gave to some guy in the Marriott bar. I remembered the street, so about a week later I looked it up and drove over there." She looked up at me briefly. "It had been a bad day."

"Tell me more about the house. He was home, I assume."

"Yes, he was home. Although not exactly thrilled to see me. He was jittery the whole time I was there, which was maybe ten minutes. I didn't realize at the time that he had a wife, one more thing he failed to mention. He couldn't wait to steer me out of there. We went to The Wine Cellar for a drink, even though it was only three in the afternoon."

"Okay, you were inside the house, right? Try to remember everything you saw."

"The place was a dump, actually. I mean, not just that it was small, but it was dirty. It smelled, and there was clutter everywhere."

"I'm trying to get a feel for the guy's lifestyle, what he did with his spare time."

"Well, he didn't clean house, that's for sure."

"Did you see any magazines laying around, any sports tickets, anything like that?"

Her eyes gazed upward, as she recreated the picture in her mind. "Newspapers," she said finally. "There were newspapers scattered everywhere. I just can't think of anything else."

It wasn't much of a start and I finally let her go, realizing that I wasn't getting much out of her. She seemed relieved, having dumped the burden of her secret in my lap. There was still a certain wariness, though. For a minute there, I wondered if she could have had something to do with Detweiller's death and was using me to find a way to cover for her.

I filed my paid bills while I tried to think what to do next. I could try to dig up some background information on Gary Detweiller so I'd have something for Ron to work on when he got back to town. I walked across the hall to Ron's office and located his Rolodex behind a tall stack of file folders. Ron isn't exactly negligent in his office duties, he just has a different system. Very different. His contact at APD is Kent Taylor in Homicide. I looked in the Rolodex under A, then under T, then under K. C for contacts didn't yield anything, either. Finally I found Taylor under P, for police. Naturally. Where else?

I phoned Taylor and got him to agree to see me at two. I didn't say why. This was an active police investigation and I knew he'd cut me off immediately if he knew I was snooping. Besides, I have much more winning ways in person than over the phone.

Sally Bertrand was at her desk when I went downstairs again for a coffee refill. She wore a pair of gray wool slacks and a blue and gray sweater. That's about as dressy as she ever gets. Usually it's jeans and plaid flannel. We run a casual operation here since Ron and I are both firm believers in jeans ourselves. Sally's shaggy blond hair was recently trimmed but not by much. I think she does it herself, probably without benefit of a mirror. She smiled at me with her wide grin, reminding me of an extra large six-year-old. She has square straight teeth, honest blue eyes, and a sprinkling of freckles across her un-madeup face.

"Who was the lady?" she asked.

"Old school friend," I answered. "You haven't seen her before because we haven't exactly been friends for about the last ten years."

"Oh." She didn't ask, and I didn't explain.

I refilled my coffee mug and carried one up front for Sally, too. She hadn't brought doughnuts, but I decided my waistline was better for it. I've been lucky all my life to never have a weight problem, but I could see that subtly changing now that I'd reached thirty. Given the facts that I love to eat and hate to exercise, something was going to have to give. When it began to give too much, I'd have to face a lifestyle change. Why don't our bodies just stay twenty-five forever?

Back in my own office, I finished up a few odds and ends. Rusty waited patiently, stretched out on a small Oriental rug near the bay window. He hadn't budged during Stacy's visit, probably thinking he'd rack up some good behavior points that way. I know the mutt. He was probably hoping for a trip to McDonalds at lunchtime. No such luck.

I worked until one, then made him stay behind when I left for my appointment with Kent Taylor. APD's headquarters is downtown, only a few blocks from our office. Getting there takes maybe ten minutes, finding a parking place, another twenty. Even so, I'd allowed myself enough time to stop along the way and indulge in a fast hamburger and Coke. In a burst of health consciousness, I skipped the fries.

Kent Taylor's office is accessed through a rabbit-warren of cubbyhole-sized spaces separated by carpet-covered dividers. Each housed a desk, chair, and wastebasket. I'd been here once before with Ron, but doubted I could find my way through the maze again. I didn't need to. I asked for Taylor at the front desk, and he came up.

Kent is a forty-ish man, dark hair thinning on top, a thick roll of extra weight around the middle. The well-fed, cared-for look of a married man with a stay-at-home wife. His pale blue shirt was neatly pressed, no spots on his tie, slacks had probably been picked up from the cleaners yesterday afternoon. I followed him back through the labyrinth to his office.

A glass wall separated his eight-by-ten space from the main room. I hadn't given much thought as to how I was going to approach him, and suddenly felt a little nervous.

"How's Ron these days?" he asked, giving me a little time to work into my story.

"Fine. He's at a firearms show right now."

"The big one in Dallas?"

I nodded. I'm uneasy about guns. Ron knows better than to push the subject with me. The gun control issue is one on which we have an ongoing debate.

The conversation with Kent was dwindling fast. If I didn't jump right in with my real question, I was going to be escorted out the door with a "nice to see you."

"What can I do for you, Charlie?" he asked.

My stomach fluttered a little. "It's about the Gary Detweiller murder. I saw the article in this morning's paper."

"Yes?"

"Well, a friend of mine knew him. He's wondering if you have any leads in the case." I don't lie easily, and I half expected Taylor to tell me so. Surely he could see the little words "Liar, Liar" popping out on my forehead.

"We have a few leads," he said. He leaned back in his chair, his fingers drumming on the arm of it. "You know how it goes, an apparently senseless killing, guy has no known enemies. But there's always a motive. Always more to the picture than the eye first sees." He fixed a direct look at me. "Why? What do you know about it?"

"Nothing, Kent. Really. I just had this friend who was concerned. Thought I'd see what I could find out."

The look of skepticism on his face stung. "Charlie, don't get involved with this. If you have a client, let Ron handle it. If your client is directly involved in this case, you better let me know all about it."

I stood up. "No, this person isn't involved with any murder," I said staunchly. I hoped it was true.

Walking the four blocks back to my Jeep, I kicked myself in the butt all the way. That had been a foolish move. All I'd accomplished was to make Kent Taylor suspicious of me. I hadn't found out a single fact about the case. And I'd come off as a meek little twit, trying to stick her nose in where it didn't belong. I felt like calling Stacy and telling her to count me out. After all, I didn't owe her a thing. She and Brad North could rot, for all I cared.

Then I remembered the look on her face, the fear that had been palpable in my office this morning. Back in our high school and college days together, Stacy and I had been close. The best of friends. We'd slept over at each other's houses almost every weekend, setting each other's hair, listening to Three Dog Night albums, giggling over boys. She'd been the only person I'd told when I lost my virginity. I'd been staying at her house the weekend my parents had flown to Denver, the weekend they never returned. Stacy's parents had been the ones to break the news of the plane crash to us. They'd held me close and taken me into their home for those first confusing weeks until my life took on some order again. The friendship with Stacy was probably what kept me from going off the deep end.

I'd been angry with her for ten years now. Losing one's fiancè to one's best friend is, if nothing else, humiliating. It was interesting, though, that in her time of need Stacy had turned to me. I wanted some time to sort this all out, but didn't have that luxury. Stacy's fear was immediate. The least I could do was try to find a few answers for her.

The past would have to be shoved into a back compartment somewhere until I could work on it. For now, I had to decide on a course of action and follow it — a more prudent course than I'd taken so far. This much intense thought called for a hot fudge sundae.

3

Thick gray clouds hung low over the Sandia Mountains. The air felt chill and smelled of moisture. Yesterday had been sunny with a sky of lapis. I was glad for my thick down jacket as I walked back to the car. A favorite memory from my high school years is hot fudge sundaes at Big Boy. With the past crowding suddenly back into my psyche today, the old craving came back. I turned east on Central Avenue.

Remodeling has changed the building somewhat, but the sundaes are the same as ever. I took a corner booth and put my feet up on the opposite seat. A few minutes later, my sundae arrived. I spooned whipped cream with a sprinkling of almonds into my mouth. I pulled my notebook out of my purse and made a few doodles in the corner. There would be something therapeutic about letting all my old feelings about Stacy and Brad flow onto the paper along with the ink from my pen but I wasn't ready for that yet. My mother had always cautioned me never to write down anything I wouldn't want to see in the newspaper. Consequently, I've never been a diary keeper. I still harbor resistance to pouring my soul out on paper. I decided to confine my notes to the murder case. Perhaps writing a plan down would help solidify a course of action for me.

Gary Detweiller. Seducer. Hangs out at country club. Wife and son. Poor neighborhood. Steals Rolex. Needs money. ???? The notes covered my small page.

I had to believe that Stacy wasn't the first woman Detweiller had seduced, probably wasn't the first he'd stolen from. His approach sounded pretty smooth, his routine well rehearsed. Except for the time Stacy had surprised him at home. Maybe his home would be a good starting place.

I scraped the last of the fudge from the bottom of the cold metal parfait cup, left too large a tip, and stepped out into the biting wind. Trotting out to the Jeep, I pulled my jacket together in front with one hand and fumbled in the pocket for my keys with the other. The clouds spat a few crumbs of snow over the hood as I started the engine. I rehearsed my story as I drove up Central, looking for the turn.

Detweiller's house was no more inviting this time, despite the addition of two cars in the driveway. A pale blue Honda held the anchor position in front of the single car garage door. The car was probably eight or nine years old, and the sun had faded the paint on the hood to near-white. Obviously, the garage held something other than the car. The second vehicle, a muscle car from the seventies, had been left primer gray with chrome pipes showing at the sides, and windows tinted so dark they were surely illegal. Stickers with illegible words drawn in sharp diagonals decorated the back window.

I pressed the doorbell, but it felt mushy and dead. When I got no response to it, I tried knocking on the screen door frame. It wobbled ineffectually, so I opened it wide enough to get my hand through, and pounded on the wooden front door. Paint flakes drifted downward.

A tired-looking woman opened the door. She was probably in her late thirties, but the eyes were aged to forty-something. Her medium brown hair was wound haphazardly around pink sponge curlers, and she clutched a limp pink robe together in front. She kept herself mostly behind the door, which she had allowed to open only about six inches.

"Mrs. Detweiller? I'm Charlie Parker. I wonder if I might speak to you about your husband."

"He's dead." So was her voice.

"I know. I'm very sorry. I just have a few questions for the investigation." The half truths were beginning to slip out more easily.

"You'd better come in," she said impatiently. "You're freezing me out, here."

She stepped back, pulling the door a bit wider. I opened the screen and stepped into the gloom. She quickly closed the door behind me. As my eyes adjusted, I could see that she wasn't wearing anything under the robe, which hung from her thin frame like a sack.

"I had just stepped out of the shower," she said. "Can you give me a minute to get dressed?"

Without waiting for an answer, she turned away. Picking up a lit cigarette from an ashtray on an end table, she disappeared into a dark hallway leaving me the perfect opportunity to check the place out.

The interior of the small house was about what I'd expected, given the looks of the exterior and what Stacy had told me about her one and only visit here. The living room where I stood was boxlike and stuffy. A tweed couch with saggy cushions, a peeling vinyl recliner, and a console stereo with a nineteen inch TV on top seemed to fill the room excessively. Decorator items were minimal — a framed print showing a dirt road winding away into the woods hung over the couch. A lump of wadded laundry, presumably clean, covered about a third of the couch. Newspapers, magazines and unopened mail were stacked on the seat of the recliner, while a couple of coats were draped over its back. One of the jackets was a man's sports coat. Hmmm...

Tentatively, I patted the pockets. A wallet sized lump rewarded my little feel-up. My heart rate picked up as I realized what I was about to do. I am not, by nature, a sneaky person. Well, maybe sneaky but I'm not dishonest. Somehow this felt dishonest.

I could hear Jean Detweiller in the bedroom. She wasn't a particularly quiet dresser. I only had a few moments, and I could think of no plausible explanation should she walk in and catch me with her husband's wallet in my hands. My stomach felt a little watery as my thumb and forefinger reached toward the pocket.

Picking through someone's wallet was better than interviewing any day. The first thing I did was to memorize Detweiller's driver's license and social security numbers. Ron had at least taught me that much about investigation. Then it was on to the good stuff. There was about thirty-five dollars cash and a condom in the money section. My, how responsible. A little sheaf of plastic windows held an insurance card, expired six months ago, a picture of a teenage boy, presumably Joshua, a coupon for a free sandwich at Subway, and some lined pages from a tiny spiral notebook, covered with angular black writing and folded in half. Somehow those leaped from the wallet to my coat pocket. In the hidden

away-from-wife's-eyes section I found a small wad
of four or five hundred dollar bills, neatly folded. It
would have probably been better politics on Gary's
part to keep the money in the money section and put
the condom here. It didn't matter now, anyway.

A noise in the hallway startled me. I dropped
the wallet back into the pocket, patted it shut,
leaped the six feet or so to stand beside the stereo,
and picked up the first newspaper my hand came to.
I was casually glancing over it when Jean Detweiller
walked back into the room. My hands were hardly
shaking at all.

"There, that's better," she said. She wore a pink
and gray waitress uniform, the kind from the fifties
where the dress is one color and the cuffs, pocket,
and collar are the other. A perky handkerchief,
folded to a point, stuck out of the pocket on her left
breast. She'd brushed out her hair and teased and
coaxed it into some kind of modified bubble. She
looked ready to report to the set of "Happy Days."
She glanced at her wristwatch.

"I've gotta be at work at four," she explained.
"Now, who did you say you are?" She continued to
bustle as she talked, apparently realizing what a
trash heap the place was.

"Charlie Parker." I avoided the real question,
figuring it was better not to tell her that I was here
at the request of her husband's latest fling. "I was
sorry to hear about your husband's death. Were you
home at the time?"

"Nope. I work six nights a week, four to mid-night, at Archie's Diner." She gathered the heap of clean laundry into her arms and headed back to the bedroom.

"Archie wouldn't let you have a few days off? I mean, considering what's happened?" I raised my voice as she left my sight.

"Oh, he would have. But what's the point?" She came back into the living room, eyeing the stack of mail and papers. "What good would it do me to sit around here for a few days?" Her voice was flat, resigned.

She picked up the mail, flipping through part of it. Apparently it was all junk, because she carried it away, presumably to the kitchen, where I heard it thunk into a trash can. I glanced at the paper I'd picked up. It was a racing form from the track down near El Paso. Quite a few entries were circled.

"Gary had been out of town, hadn't he?"

"Yeah, I think so. I didn't keep tabs on the man," she said wearily. "I tried that in the early years, but it's just too, you know, too draining. Gary gambled, he drank, he cheated. Nothin' I said or did was gonna change that."

"Why didn't you just boot him out?"

"I guess for Josh's sake. Gary didn't give a lot, but having him around did help keep Josh under control. Do you know what a single mother has to cope with these days? Especially with a teenage boy?"

"I saw two cars out there. Is Josh home?"

"He's asleep. Stayed home from school today. He's taken this pretty hard, and I don't think he slept at all last night."

She had tidied up the room quite a bit while we talked, but I imagined her son would return it to its previous condition by the time she got home. I noticed that she avoided touching her husband's coat, which still lay across the back of the recliner. She glanced at her watch again, giving me my cue.

I drove away wondering what, exactly, I had learned. The thick gray clouds still blanketed the city, blending with the streets, sidewalks, and barren trees. The effect was like driving through a scene on black and white television where only the cars and billboards have been colorized. The sleet-like granules had disappeared. It would be rare to have any lasting snowfall in town this late in the season. Afternoon traffic was beginning to pick up, and it took me almost thirty minutes to get to the office.

Rusty was waiting at the back door anxiously. Sally had left hours ago, and with no one else there he had probably begun to wonder if he was abandoned. His thick tail whapped against the doorframe as I unlocked it. He took about ten seconds to sniff my hands and give me a couple of doggy kisses before racing to the back yard to avail himself of the facilities.

I checked the answering machine and Sally's

desk. No messages. My desk was similarly clear, so
I closed the shades, double checked the locks and
left, guilt-free.

The stolen notes from Gary Detweiller's wallet
were burning a hole in my pocket and I could hardly
wait to get a look at them. Fortunately, the traffic
accommodated me. It was considerably lighter this
side of town. Unfortunately, my next door neighbor
was not quite that accommodating. She met me in
my driveway.

Elsa Higgins is eighty-six years old, practically
a grandmother to me. In fact, I call her Gram because Mrs. Higgins seems too formal and calling an
older woman by her first name was unthinkable in
my mother's eyes. So, from my earliest memories,
Elsa has been Gram to me. She's feisty and opinion-
ated and I want to be just like her when I grow up.
We've been neighbors all my life. She lives alone in
the same house she's occupied for more than forty
years, where she does all the cooking, cleaning and
gardening. She took me in when my parents died,
letting me live with her for probably the two most
difficult years in anyone's life, age sixteen to eighteen. That's when I decided I was grown up enough
to take care of myself, so I moved back into my own
house. I grew up here and my parents left the house
to me, so I found no reason to go elsewhere. I still
haven't.

The neighborhood is one of the older ones in
town, the Albuquerque Country Club area. It's situ-

ated near Old Town, the site of the original Albuquerque, now an official historic district complete with adobe buildings, a town square and tourist trap prices. Our residential area is just far enough away to avoid the traffic and tourists. The homes are not elaborate by today's standards, but they have a certain charm, including tall old trees and neatly clipped lawns. My place is typical, a three-bedroom ranch style white brick with hardwood floors. I have it furnished with oriental rugs and antiques. The back yard has fifty-foot tall sycamores and my mother's peace roses. No, I wouldn't trade it for a trendy little townhouse in Tanoan.

I pulled the Jeep to a quick stop in the driveway, and Rusty and I both hopped out.

"Gram, you better get inside before you freeze!" She was wearing polyester slacks and blouse, with only a thin cardigan over it.

"Oh, I'm okay, Charlie. I only stepped outside when I saw your car coming up the street." She shivered anyway, though, so I put my arm around her small shoulders and guided her to the door. Inside, the heat was a welcome relief.

"Is anything wrong?" I asked. Meeting me at the car in freezing weather was not exactly Elsa's style.

"Paul's coming," she breathed.

"Paul, my brother? When did this happen?"

"He called me this afternoon. Said he couldn't reach either you or Ron, and wanted to be sure you'd be home this weekend."

"*This* weekend? Oh, boy."

"Why? Will you be gone?"

"Oh, no, I'll be here." The enthusiasm in my voice was about zero point one on the Richter scale. "I wonder why he called you. I was at the office most of the day."

She shrugged. She stands all of five foot two, which puts her shoulders about chest-high to me. Second-guessing Paul is futile. He's not irresponsible, understand, just unpredictable. Of the three of us, he *appears* to be the most solid. Married to his original spouse, two kids, churchgoers all, a respectable job with a computer firm. We don't have a lot in common.

Ron and I, on the other hand, tend to barrel through life, seeking our own way. Although Ron did the marriage bit once, and I never have, he and I have more of a kindred feeling than either of us share with Paul. Like this making of weekend plans on a Thursday, then going into a panic when he couldn't reach anyone. No doubt he'd left messages on both Ron's and my home answering machines, but did he think to call the office where we'd likely be during the day?

I turned to Elsa again. "Would you like a cup of tea?" I asked, deciding I could look at Gary Detweiller's papers later.

"Yes, that would be nice," she answered.

She followed me into the kitchen, where I put water on to boil and looked for cups. My mother's collection of delicate china teacups sits unused most of the time, so I chose a couple of especially pretty ones, delicately flowered. There was half a Sara Lee poundcake in the fridge, so I sliced it and got out raspberry jam. We might as well make a real tea out of it. Elsa doesn't get out much.

"Will Paul's family stay here when they visit?" she asked, eyeing the poundcake slices even though the water wasn't hot yet.

"I guess so. Ron's apartment has only one bedroom. Usually Paul and Lorraine stay in my guest room, and we make up pallets on the floor in my office for the kids."

The image of letting two permissively raised kids spend time in my home office made me think of all the stuff I'd have to hide first. Annie and Joe aren't purposely destructive, just presumptuous. At home they have access to everything on the premises without asking. I'm not that gracious with my things.

The water boiled and I went through the ritual of preheating the teapot, steeping the bags precisely five minutes, and pouring. I never do this just for myself, but I enjoyed giving Elsa the extra attention. The stolen papers could wait. I might not have Gram around that much longer. We each helped ourselves to two slices of cake, and since there was an extra, I coaxed her to take the last one. Thirty minutes later, I watched her safely across the narrow expanse of yard that separates her house from mine.

After checking the mail (two bills, eight pieces of junk) and the answering machine (one message from you-know-who), I finally sat down at the kitchen table with Gary Detweiller's neat little notebook pages. They were in some kind of code.

4

Neat rows of letters and numbers covered the pages, written in bold black strokes. Entries like 3B5T-94-157, 3C4P-96-782, and 8T9Z-19-853 filled line after line. I poured another cup of tea and stared at the numbers as if some magical pattern might appear. There was a pattern all right, but I sure couldn't see the magic in it.

I tried to make them into dates and times. The 94 and 96 might be dates, but 19? 157 might be a time, but 782? On a yellow notepad, I rewrote them in other sequences, but didn't come up with anything that way, either. The letters could clearly be initials, but finding BT, CP, and TZ in the phone directory would obviously be futile.

The ringing telephone interrupted me just about the time I was getting frustrated anyway.

"Charlie, I'm so glad I finally reached you!" Paul sounded like he was about to impart some tragic news.

"Gram told me you're coming to town this weekend. Is there some emergency?"

"No." He sounded puzzled. "Just wanted to let you know we're coming."

"Driving or flying?"

"Driving." That was okay with me. Flying meant I'd have to pick them up at the airport. Of course, driving meant they'd pull in late at night, so I'd either have to wait up or leave them a key.

"Just you, or everyone?"

"All of us."

"Great." Great.

"Well, I'll see you when?"

"Probably late Friday night."

"Good, I'll see you then." He hung up.

Most of Paul's conversations go this way. With Ron, I seem to always have things to say. Maybe it's because we work together, I'm not sure. We've always been close, though. Ron is the oldest; as a kid he was my protector. Paul's in the middle. Maybe there's something to that middle child thing. I should read up on it sometime. One nice thing about Paul's visits — he and Lorraine have plenty of old friends in town to see besides me.

It was beginning to get dark outside, so I turned

on a few lamps and closed the drapes. I re-read the
newspaper article on the murder. The shots had
been heard by a neighbor around nine, and the
police arrived at the scene about nine-twenty. I
studied the fuzzy picture of Detweiller, which, judging by the hairstyle and clothing, had to be at least
ten years old. Longish dark hair and heavy side-
burns past the earlobes framed a boyish face. The
lopsided smile exuded sex. Dark hair sprouted from
the open collar of his shirt. Even in the blurred photo
a cocky attitude came through. I honestly thought
Stacy had better taste.

Still full from tea, I decided not to bother with
dinner. I spent another hour staring at Gary's numbers, but gave it up in favor of a movie on TV. It's an
escape technique, I know, but I still wasn't ready to
examine my own feelings about Stacy, Brad and this
whole situation.

My bedside clock said it was three-oh-eight
when I woke from an apparently sound sleep with
the answer. The codes were names and phone numbers. And it wasn't even that tricky. I pulled on a
robe and went to the kitchen. Florescent light is
nearly unbearable at three a.m. but I couldn't wait.
I ripped the top sheet off the yellow pad to expose a
clean page. I wrote down each of the numbers in
reverse sequence and moved the letters to the end.
Sure enough, they were all Albuquerque prefixes.
The dashes had apparently been placed to confuse
the casual looker. I would bet money that I'd find

each of these numbers when I checked them tomorrow in our criss-cross directory at the office.

Rusty had followed me into the kitchen, worried that I might be indulging in a late-night snack without him. When no food appeared, he satisfied himself by drinking about a quart of water from his bowl, then dribbling half of it across the floor. I wiped up the spots, then we both headed back to bed. I slept like a dead person until seven.

By ten o'clock, I'd looked up all the phone numbers on the code sheets. As I'd suspected, the two-letter combination with each matched a name. I was feeling like quite the investigator. All I had to do now was figure out whether this had any relevance at all to Detweiller's death.

I thought of the racing form I'd seen at the house. Stupid of me not to steal that, too, as long as I was now heavy into thievery. Detweiller obviously liked to play the horses, and the fact that he carried a list of names and phone numbers around in code made me think he might be doing a little bookmaking. I'd written down complete names and addresses to go with the phone numbers on the coded list. There was quite a variety here. Some of the addresses were in very affluent parts of town. One of them might even be a neighbor of Stacy's. I'd have to check that out. Maybe Gary's chance meeting with her at the country club hadn't been pure chance after all.

"What's up?" Sally stood in my doorway, laughing at how she'd just about startled me out of my chair.

"I'm working on a case. For Stacy North."

"A case? Isn't that Ron's department?" Then my words really registered. "For Stacy North! As in Brad North? As in heartbreak of the century?"

"Don't overdramatize. That was ten years ago, my heart wasn't broken, just mildly cracked, and from what I'm learning now, I think I have a lot to thank Stacy for."

"You're *kidding*."

"Unh-unh." I began to realize that this conversation wasn't exactly discreet, so I busied myself shuffling the papers around, covering up any vital evidence in the process.

"Look, what I really stopped in for was to see if you'd like to go backpacking with Ross and me this weekend. We're going down to the Gila." She tried to make it sound like Disneyland.

"Gee, I uh.. I can't. Paul and Lorraine and the kids are coming." I hoped I sounded properly regretful. Truthfully, I'd rather have a root canal.

"Well, maybe some other time." She breezed away, feelings apparently intact.

A pile of correspondence waited to be answered, but I couldn't get my mind off Detweiller. Who wanted him dead? At this point I didn't have enough information to hazard a guess. I thought about interviewing all the people on my list. There must have been forty names, an awesome task as-

suming that any of them would even talk to me. I
tried to think of a logical place to begin.

Motive, means, opportunity. The three key
words in finding a criminal. What I needed at this
point were more facts. I called Stacy at home, sug-
gesting lunch. She recommended the club, and I said
I'd come by her house to pick her up. She gave me
directions. I wasn't sure what had prompted my
offer to come to her house. I'd never had the least
curiosity about her life with Brad but now I wondered. Maybe I'd gain some insight into the friend I
hadn't seen in so long.

I organized my desk and watered all the plants
in the office before leaving. Rusty stayed behind to
keep Sally company. I dashed home to change
clothes before starting the trek to the far northeast
heights. I'd never been inside the Tanoan Country
Club, and hoped that an emerald green dress with
soft wool draped flatteringly across the bodice would
be appropriate. The color set off my auburn hair
nicely anyway. I chucked the down jacket for a calf
length wool coat that I hadn't worn in ten years and
hoped it wasn't too far out of style.

The temperature was in the fifties, with a clear
sky the color of a robin's egg. I was no sooner in the
car than I decided the wool coat would have to go. I
couldn't handle the bulk or the warmth. Outside, I
could stand it but not in here. The Tanoan community is just about as far away as one can get from
the side of town where I live — geographically and

mentally. Surrounded by white walls the observer gets glimpses of what would probably be stately homes if they weren't packed so tightly together. From the outside the impression is lots of earthtone stucco, windows, balconies, and Spanish tile, jammed into a conglomeration that makes it difficult to know where one house begins and the other ends. Each of these architectural delights needs a minimum of two acres to show it off properly. Instead, they are crammed onto regular city lots. And to think they pay extra for this coziness.

I turned left at the first break in the big white wall. A matching white guardhouse was planted into the middle of the drive, with hefty-looking black iron gates on either side. The gate leading in stood open, but a guard with folded arms waited, daring me to drive through without stopping. On the other side, the exit, fearsome tire spikes awaited any who might attempt gate running through the "outie." I wasn't sure I wanted in at all, certainly not badly enough to pay for four flat tires.

I pulled to a stop beside the guard. On closer inspection, he was at least seventy, with a big toothless grin that wasn't the least bit scary. I told him where I was going and he waved me through. His smile remained the same throughout, and I wondered whether he even heard my words.

The North home was about three blocks into the rabbit warren of curving streets. Stacy had given good directions. I found the three story wonder, despite the fact that stylewise it was very much like three-fourths of its neighbors. Light tan stucco, broken by two balconies across the front, long windows, curved at the top, and a mahogany door inset with beveled glass. Every window was curtained in white sheers, which appealed to my sense of neatness, but they also gave the place a sense of separation, of being locked away from the world. I tried to imagine these people having a pathway through the hedge to the elderly neighbor with whom they'd had a lifelong grandmotherly relationship. But their hedges were made of unyielding block walls, perfectly stuccoed to match their perfect houses. Most of the people were high powered two-career families who worked ninety hours a week to afford their affluence.

I touched a button beside the door, setting off a pealing of chimes. Stacy opened the door moments later. She wore white wool slacks and a turtleneck sweater that looked like it was made of cotton candy. Her hair and makeup were perfect, although her smile was a little stiff. I gathered that she had completely recovered from Gary Detweiller's death and now wanted to pretend he never existed.

"Well, Stace, you guys have really made it big." I gazed around at the foyer. Apparently, it was the reaction she expected. Her smile warmed up as she offered to show me around. I oohed and aahed at the appropriate times as she led me through eighteen rooms of mauve carpet, mauve wallcoverings, and mauve tile. The brag wall in the study was covered with framed certificates proclaiming Brad the Outstanding Young Attorney of the Year several years running. Photos of Stacy and Brad standing next to various politicians and movie stars broke up the monotony of the certificates. Wide smiles and cocktail glasses were the prevailing theme and many of the photos were signed by the famous member of the group, usually with some very sincere preface like Love Ya... or Kisses... I found myself saying things like "Well, well," and "Would you look at that" over and over. We did about fifteen minutes of this routine before I got a long enough break to remind her about lunch.

To reach the Tanoan County Club, we exited the community through the guard post where I'd come in, onto Academy Road. Less than a mile up the road another turn-in opened past another guard gate onto a winding lane leading to yet another stucco and red tiled structure. Inside, the carpet cushed under our feet as we mushed our way past a receptionist and up a wide staircase to the restaurant on the second floor.

The maitre d' greeted Stacy with just the right combination of familiarity and genuflection. I stood by, practicing Stacy's slightly drooped mouth and half lowered eyelids, wondering if I'd ever have a need to learn country club protocol. We followed *Andre*, whose real name was probably Andy, to a corner table where windows on two sides gave the full sweeping view of the city. Right now it was a panoramic display of gray, topped by a frosting of brown air. Well, maybe it was spectacular at night.

We perused the menu and placed our orders before I got a chance to get down to the real reason for the lunch date.

"I guess you figured out that I wanted to update you on the case," I began. "So far, I haven't learned a lot. Apparently Gary was into gambling pretty heavily. I'm going to work on that angle first."

Stacy shushed me briefly while the waiter brought our salads.

"I don't want anyone here to connect me with that man," she whispered. "You know how staff people can be."

I wanted to shake this uppity attitude right out of her but I let it slide. "Do you know anything about Gary's movements on Wednesday?" I asked. "I'm trying to put together a picture that leads to him sitting in his car in the driveway at nine that night."

"Absolutely not." Her voice rose four notes. "I had nothing whatsoever to do with the man after he took my watch."

"Okay, okay." I patted the tablecloth near her hand. "I just have to ask the questions. Stacy, where were you at nine o'clock on Wednesday?"

"Charlie!" A couple of heads turned, and she lowered her voice immediately. "What are you getting at?"

"Stacy, you better face facts. The police might be

asking that very question if they ever make the connection with you. You better be ready with an answer."

She chewed at her salad slowly before speaking again. "That was the night Brad got home from his business trip. I picked him up at the airport. The flight came in at nine-thirty. That's where I was."

I fixed a long look on her. I wanted to believe her, but it was entirely possible for a person to be at Detweiller's house at nine, then beat it to the airport by nine-thirty to meet a plane. She sat up very straight and returned my stare.

"Charlie, I'm telling you, I was at the airport."

"Okay." I let it drop. We ate in silence for a few minutes before changing the subject. When I dropped her off at her house thirty minutes later, I couldn't resist adding one more word of caution.

"Stacy, if you have any proof at all to back up your airport story, I suggest you get it ready. I have a feeling the police are going to want to see it."

I glanced back in my rearview mirror as I pulled out of her circular drive. She stood on the front porch, glued to the spot, her face pale.

5

At the intersection of Academy and Wyoming, I pulled into a grocery store parking lot. Pulling my yellow sheet of notes from my purse, I reviewed the names I'd compiled this morning. According to my city map, two of the addresses were in the Tanoan Community. I headed east on Academy once more. This time the guard waved me right on through with a little salute, like I was a resident. I found the address for Charles Tompkins with no trouble. The house looked like an elder sibling of Stacy's place. Obviously they'd come from the same gene pool. The place looked deserted and the cascade of pealing chimes brought no one. I got the same non-response at the second address I tried.

Still only two o'clock. I didn't particularly feel like sitting around another three or four hours until the residents came home. Plus, I imagined anyone sitting in a car in this neighborhood, day or night, would attract attention from the roving patrol I'd seen cruising the area.

Detweiller's place was sort of on my way back to the office, so I thought I'd see if I could catch Josh Detweiller at home. I got half-lucky. His mother's car was also in the drive. Jean was sure to question me more closely if I showed up twice in two days. That wouldn't do. I cruised past the place and stopped about four houses away. Rearview mirror surveillance is neither easy nor inconspicuous, requiring a person to keep their head and neck in one position for hours. After about twenty minutes I decided I had to turn around. I started the Jeep and drove to the next driveway where I could make a turn. Just as I was getting positioned again, this time facing the correct way down the street, I noticed activity at the Detweiller house.

Jean Detweiller emerged from the front door, turning to speak back to it. Last minute instructions for Josh, I imagined. She proceeded toward her car, rummaging in her purse and not paying much attention to anything else. She started the car, gunning it loudly while a puff of gray smoke whoofed from the tailpipe. The car clunked into gear with a jerk and she backed out carefully, turning in my direction. I ducked down in my seat until her car passed me, praying she didn't remember my vehicle from yesterday.

When the coast was clear I drove up to the house, hoping Jean had left for work and not some quick errand. Rock music thumped heavy bass clear out to the street. Obviously Josh didn't expect his mother right back. I pounded on the door twice, realizing the futility of it. I waited for a break between songs, then pounded again. The music came back on, about a hundred decibels lower this time, and the door opened.

Josh Detweiller was almost a double for a very young Elvis. Except for the hair, which he wore chin length, the sultry face was nearly identical. He wore faded blue jeans, nothing else, and the sight of his smooth muscular chest was most distracting.

"Josh?" My voice finally began working. "Hi, I'm Charlie."

"Hi." His grin reassured me that I'm not completely over the hill.

"I'm investigating your father's death," I explained, flashing one of RJP Investigations' business cards. I didn't offer to leave the card with him.

"Oh. Come in." He pushed the screen door outward and stepped back. He was pulling a t-shirt over his head when I got in.

"This must be hard for you," I said. "Your mother said you stayed home from school for a few days."

He shrugged.

"Look, I don't have a lot to go on, but I'm trying to find out who did it. Can you tell me what happened that night?"

"I dunno," he said. He disappeared into his room for a minute and shut off the music. "I wasn't even here when it happened. I came home about midnight and Mom was all shook up and she was crying and all, and that's when she told me."

"You'd been out with your friends?"

"Yeah, a coupla guys from school."

"Your dad had been out of town, right?"

"I think so. Coupla days, I guess." His face contorted with anger. "Hell, I don't keep track of him. Nobody did. He was probably out with some chick in some fancy hotel someplace. I don't give a shit." He slumped and turned his face slightly. "Sorry."

"It's okay, Josh. You gotta say what's on your mind."

He flopped down on the couch, oblivious to the pile of newspapers he was crunching. I perched on the arm of the vinyl recliner.

"Did you and your dad get along pretty well?" I tried to ask the question kindly.

". . . Oh, okay, I guess. Dad did a lot of macho image shit. You know, he bragged all the time, played the ponies. He always, you know, dreamed about hitting it big. Couldn't just have a job like everyone else's dad, bring home a paycheck every week. He was always chasing some gold mine. Always thought he'd make a million next week. It just gets old hearing it, you know."

"Your mom was pretty tolerant of all this, wasn't she?"

He huffed a sharp breath out his nose. "What choice did she have? My mom works hard." He pointed his index finger, stabbing at the sofa cushion. "But she still doesn't make enough to get us out of this rat trap."

"Can you think of anyone with a reason to kill your dad?"

He shrugged again. "Maybe lots of people. Hell, I stayed away from most of his friends. Well, his one friend really. This guy Larry Burke. A slimeball. Just like Dad."

He stood up and disappeared into his room again. I thought he was coming right back, but the music came back on loud again and I realized that was all I'd get from Josh Detweiller. I let myself out.

I keep a set of phone books in my car, so I checked out Larry Burke. His address was only a couple of streets away. It was still a little early for anyone who worked a nine-to-five job to be home, but I decided to take my chances. The Burke house was a little larger than the Detweiller place, but in about the same condition. A gum-popping redhead answered the door. She wore black Lycra pants and a luminescent pink top that might have been applied to her model-thin body with a vacuum sealer. Her makeup looked freshly done, like the "after" in one of those makeover ads. Unfortunately, she was made over to look twenty when she was really closer to forty.

"Mrs. Burke?" I asked.

She gave me a blank look.

"Excuse me, I'm looking for Larry Burke. Is this his residence?" The smell of frying onions wafted out around her.

"He ain't home." More gum action.

"When will he be back?"

Her eyes narrowed as she checked me out head to toe. "Who wants to know?" Oh, please. She couldn't honestly believe I was after him for personal reasons.

"I'm looking into Gary Detweiller's death," I explained. "Larry was his best friend, wasn't he?"

"I don't know when he'll be home," she said. "He don't answer to me." She closed the door in my face.

Some help that was. No answers, and I was getting hungrier by the minute. My nine dollar salad at lunch sure wasn't sticking with me. There was a McDonald's about three blocks away, so I set my course in that direction. The driveup window yielded a Big Mac, Coke, and fries, which I sampled on my way back to Larry Burke's house. That floozy didn't honestly think she'd get rid of me that easily, did she?

I parked two houses south of theirs and proceeded with my little picnic. By the time I'd licked the last of the special sauce from my fingers the temperature had begun to drop. My ankles were really feeling it. Wearing a dress, pantyhose, and heels is not my usual style. I kicked off the shoes and tucked my legs up under me, wrapping the wool coat securely around myself.

Lights came on in the surrounding houses, and one by one cars pulled into driveways. A streetlight glowed almost a block away. I snuggled deeper into my coat. I thought about Rusty, waiting at the office, which would now be dark. What was I doing here anyway?

I had just decided I was being foolish and had reached for my shoes when a car pulled into Burke's drive. It was a sports car of some kind, flashier than anything I'd seen so far in the neighborhood. The brakes gave a little squeal as he stopped about six inches from the garage door. I came out of my car before he had a chance to disappear.

"Mr. Burke? Could I talk to you a second?" I was almost breathless from dashing the length of two houses. He stopped in his driveway and looked at me curiously.

Larry Burke was about five foot six, slender, wearing a pair of dark slacks and plaid polyester sports coat. His blond hair looked like it had been molded from polystyrene. When he moved, it stayed in place. He had straight capped teeth, which showed through a well-practiced grin. I was reminded of a TV evangelist or a cookware salesman.

In the time it took me to cross his driveway, he had checked me over twice.

"Hey, babe, what can I do for you?" The voice was like thick grease.

I do not take well to being called babe, honey, sweetie, or dear by someone I do not know intimately. My teeth clenched and my smile became a straight line.

"Charlie Parker, RJP Investigations," I said as officiously as I could manage. "I've been asked to look into the death of Gary Detweiller."

Burke shifted his weight from one foot to the other, backing away from me a couple of feet.

"Yeah, that was a shame about ol' Gare."

"You were his best friend, I understand."

"We hung around, yeah." He implied nothing as sentimental as real friendship, I noted.

"When did you see him last?"

"Prob'ly just before it happened. We'd gone to Vegas for a coupla days, got back Wednesday night, and he dropped me off here. Guess it was right after that somebody got him."

"What were you doing in Vegas?"

"Just fun stuff. Gary'd come into some money, so we celebrated. Went to the races, ate in some good restaurants, partied with a couple of babes." He glanced toward the front door as he revealed this last part.

"Where'd he get the money?" I asked, wondering

just how far he'd let me go with these questions
before he closed up.

"Said he managed a big score. I don't know, I
wasn't his mother. Gary and me was like that. We
shared the wealth. When one of us got lucky, we took
the other one along."

"So, who'd want to kill him?"

"Hell, I don't know. Gary was a good guy, you
know, liked to have some fun. He didn't mean nobody no harm, though. I mean, you know, he'd get
involved with some chick from time to time. For him
it was just fun, somethin' to do with somebody new.
I guess sometimes they got a little pissed when he
didn't stick around."

Or when he ripped them off.

He kept glancing toward the front door, probably wondering how long until the redhead came
sailing out with claws extended. No doubt she'd
heard his car arrive.

"Look, thanks," I said. I gave him one of my
business cards and asked him to call if he thought
of anything else.

Back in the car, I started the engine and let the
heater warm up. I wondered again how many
women Detweiller had robbed over the years. Was
Stacy only the latest, or had he kept several going
at once? I wished I'd asked Burke a few more
questions. Maybe later.

I drove as quickly as I could to the office, where
Rusty greeted me like I'd been gone years. We

headed home, where I rewarded his patience with a bowl of nuggets followed by a rawhide chew. For myself, my reward was to strip off the pantyhose and slip into snugly sweats. I made a cup of hot chocolate, prepared to sink into the sofa cushions and ponder all the new information I'd gathered today. Until I remembered that I'd have houseguests sometime around midnight.

I dusted the guest room and put extra towels in the guest bath. My office required a little more screening. Everything that might appeal to kids, such as calculator, computer, and stapler either went into locked file drawers or got covered up. A box of games and puzzles, which I keep in the closet for such occasions, came out. I hoped it would provide enough distraction to keep the little critters out of my own stuff. I checked my supply of extra blankets and pillows, just in case they forgot to bring their own sleeping bags. I took one last look around and hoped I was ready.

6

By two a.m. I had dozed off on the couch, having watched all the TV movies I could handle. The magic hour of midnight had long passed, leaving me grumpy at this interruption of my schedule. Going to sleep knowing you could be awakened at any moment does not exactly make for restful slumber. Three hard raps at the front door, followed by giggles, snapped me awake. I rubbed at my grainy eyes and ran my fingers through my hair on the way to the door.

"Rusty! Rusty!" Two balls of energy bounded through the door, intent on the object of their affection. The poor dog tried to take refuge behind my legs and we ended up with a tangle of bodies that almost sent all of us to the floor.

"Hi, Sis." Paul greeted me with a dry kiss on the cheek. He carried two suitcases and had two sleeping bags hanging from his shoulders by straps.

"We got away later than we'd planned," Lorraine explained, not sounding nearly apologetic enough for waking me at two a.m. Her arms loaded with brown grocery sacks, she pushed her way through the tangle of kids and dog toward the kitchen. Paul headed to the guest room without stopping, apparently worried about losing his momentum with the heavy load.

Three minutes later we were all assembled in the living room.

"Would anyone like hot chocolate?" I offered. I noticed they were all wearing light cotton clothing. Lorraine was visibly shivering.

"Yea, chocolate," Annie and Joe shrieked at once.

"They slept most of the way here," Paul explained. "I guess they're getting their second wind." No kidding.

"Why don't you kids check out the games in your room," I suggested. "I'll call you when the hot chocolate's ready." I turned to Lorraine. "Is that everything from the car?" She nodded.

Paul and Lorraine followed me into the kitchen, with Rusty sticking close to my legs. I found packets

of instant hot chocolate mix in a cupboard and
rounded up mugs while the water heated.

"So, how is Phoenix these days?" I asked.

"Fine, fine. Getting warm already."

I'd never known a time when Phoenix wasn't
warm. The end of February should be no exception.

"How's the job?" I thought I could see a hint of
gray at my brother's temples.

"Fine, fine."

Lorraine piped up. "Paul had a promotion last
month," she said.

The conversation continued in this lively vein
until we'd finished off the hot chocolate and I
couldn't keep my eyes open another minute. We
finally got the kids settled into their sleeping bags,
although they didn't look the least bit sleepy. I went
to bed wondering what we'd find to talk about for
the next two days.

I found Paul wandering in the backyard at eight
the next morning. Everyone else was still asleep. He
slipped his arm around my shoulders as we walked
among the dried stalks of last summer's flowers.
The earth smelled faintly damp. I noticed the young
green shoots of daffodils and tulips had grown noticeably taller in the past couple of days.

"Lorraine wants to visit her friend from college,
Betsy Royce, today," Paul said. "Betsy's kids are
about the same age as Annie and Joe. I think they'll
have a good time together."

"You going too?"

"Would you mind? Jack Royce and I were pretty good friends."

"No, I don't mind. You guys make your plans. I've got things to do. Want to meet back here for dinner?"

"Pedro's?"

"You got it." Pedro's is a little Mexican food place, just far enough away from the tourist traffic that it hasn't lost its charm. I eat there a couple of times a week. Pedro and his wife, Concha, make the best sour cream chicken enchiladas in the state, and their margaritas are fantastic.

I puttered in the kitchen, pondering where I'd go next with the Detweiller case, wondering if I was going to be in a ton of trouble for pursuing it on my own. I'd have to bring Ron up to date on it the minute he got back to town. The thought occurred to me that I might have better luck reaching some of those names on Gary's list on a Saturday. After feeding my guests a hearty breakfast of cold cereal and seeing them out the door, I pulled out the list once again.

About half the names came from the same part of town where Detweiller had lived. Probably neighbors, co-workers, guys he'd met in neighborhood bars. The other half of the list contained a variety, a surprising number located in well-off parts of town. I wasn't sure where I'd get the most information, from the average working-guy types or from the successful ones who might have gotten tricked into the association with Gary, much as Stacy had.

I stopped at the first gas station to fill up. This might end up being a long day. The Jeep took fourteen gallons, which I put on the credit card we use for company expenses. I'd decided to try the upper-crust neighborhood first. Two of the addresses were in Tanoan, so I headed out I-25 to the San Mateo exit, then up Academy Road. The guard today was a different one, and I hadn't really thought about what my approach would be. I doubted they routinely let in investigators who want to question their residents. Especially when the investigator was really an accountant. My only choice would be to fake it. I told the guard I was going to Stacy North's house, hoping all the while that he wouldn't call her to verify it.

He didn't. He waved me through like his main concern in the world was what time he'd get off work. I drove straight to one of the houses where I'd gotten no answer yesterday. The place still looked closed up tight. A newspaper rested on the front step. I rang the doorbell without much hope, and was startled when a sleepy-looking man in silk pajamas opened it.

The man looked almost as startled at seeing me. His curly blond hair stuck out at angles and his pajama top was skewed off to one side. He blinked at the sunlight, trying to focus on my face.

"Charles Tompkins?"

"Who are you?" If I'd been an attacker, he would have been an extremely easy mark.

"My name's Charlie Parker. Do you know a Gary Detweiller?"

"Who?"

"Gary Detweiller. Your bookie."

He suddenly stood very still. His eyes had no trouble focusing directly on mine now. A white rim showed around the edges of his thin lips.

"I don't know who you are, or who you're looking for, lady, but you got the wrong address." His hand had moved to the edge of the door.

"Fine. Detweiller's dead, and I imagine the next ones to come knocking at your door will be the police." I turned away. "Have a nice day," I said sweetly.

"Uh . . . wait. What did you say your name was?" He had removed his hand from the door. I noticed a sheen on his forehead.

"Charlie Parker. RJP Investigations. Someone else with, shall we say, a not exactly legitimate connection to Detweiller has asked me to look into his death. This person is another Tanoan resident. With the information I've found so far, I suspect Detweiller had targeted you folks, figuring he'd found a gold mine."

"Look," he glanced behind me nervously, "why don't you come inside a minute."

I stepped into a cool white hall, from which I could see a white living room on one side and a white dining room on the other. The chrome and glass furnishings didn't add any color. Only brief dashes of black accent pieces kept me aware that I hadn't fallen into a snowbank.

"Excuse me a minute," Tompkins said, walking up a staircase to my right. He returned two minutes later, slipping his arms into a paisley silk robe. He hadn't combed his curls.

We took seats in the chilly living room. Tompkins reclined in a puffy down-cushioned chair. He couldn't maintain the pose, though. He fidgeted, crossing and re-crossing his legs, scooting to the edge of his seat.

"Now what about this man, what was the name?"

"Detweiller." Don't play ignorant with me, bud.

"Yes, now who was he?"

I stared at his face for a full minute, while his eyes darted around the room.

"How much did Detweiller take you for?" I finally asked.

"What makes you think. . ." He drew himself up defensively.

"I think Detweiller was a schemer and a con man. He worked his way into his victim's confidence, then took whatever he could. With the women, he used sex, with the men, I imagine there was some kind of money scheme. He played the horses a lot. Maybe that was it with you."

"Horse racing? I hardly think so," Tompkins tone was scathing.

"What, then?" I stayed patient, letting him think about it. Two or three plans crossed his mind. I watched them play out rapidly.

"Okay," he finally said. "You're right. It was an investment scheme. And oddly enough it did involve horses." He chuckled dryly. "I met Detweiller in the Card Room at the club. He wasn't a member. I was pretty sure of that. I assumed he was there as a guest. We got to talking. I've always been fascinated by horse racing. Not so much as a bettor. I was interested in the horses themselves, the breeding, the bloodlines. Gary picked up on that and told me he'd done a lot of investing in race horses. Said he could get me into this consortium that had already bought into some of the finest champions in the country. He knew all the names, their records."

"Because he hung around the tracks all the time."

"I found that out later. This guy was smooth."

I thought of the picture I'd seen of Detweiller. I couldn't see how a well-off man like this wouldn't have seen right through the facade. Then again, why hadn't Stacy seen through it either? Maybe Detweiller was a chameleon.

"And you ended up losing your money," I suggested.

"Twenty thousand. He had me thinking I was

one of the small investors, too — that most of them were putting in hundreds."

"So, when did you find out the whole thing was a sham?"

"Just now, really. I'd been calling Gary for a week, wondering when I would get some word about the investment. I was supposed to get reports, statements, and so forth. It had been over a month since I'd given him the money and I was getting concerned. I'd called for several days in a row, and was really starting to get mad."

Mad enough to kill? I wondered.

"Now wait a minute," he protested, reading my thoughts. "Yeah, I was mad that he was ignoring my calls. But twenty thousand dollars is not enough to kill for. An embarrassment, maybe, but not worth risking my neck over."

I believed him. Twenty thou was a new decorating job for the living room to this guy. He wasn't going to risk this lifestyle over a man of Detweiller's caliber.

Back in the car, I considered visiting the other names I had whose addresses were in this area. But I had the feeling I'd get the same story. Whatever scheme Gary had used with each of them, the bottom line was not financial ruin. Poor Gary Detweiller, for all his illusions of importance, was nothing more than an embarrassment to these people.

Which brought me to consider the other half of

the list. What about those working class slobs who might have sunk all they had into one of Detweiller's schemes?

7

"Gary? Sure, Gary Detweiller was a friend of mine. Do anything for ya, he would." A grease-encrusted hand reached out from under the hood of the sixty-three Chevy, groping for an open end wrench.

I'd driven across town to one of the other addresses on my list. Zack Taylor lived little more than a dozen blocks from Detweiller's home. The house was an average sized ranch style home with a gray shingled pitched roof and red brick front. The double wide garage door stood open, so I'd walked on in.

Taylor was bent over the engine of the old car, like a surgeon in the midst of a delicate operation. The hood had been removed, leaving the patient's innards exposed. A hundred watt drop light hung from the rafters. Tools waited like surgical instruments, lined up on a towel which also served to protect the fender on which they rested. The remainder of the garage was filled with tires, boxes, bicycles, and the other assorted stuff that usually preempt a car from occupying the second space.

Zack Taylor was probably in his late twenties, old enough to have a family, judging by the junk in the garage, but not old enough to have given up his stock race car. A hole in the garage where you pour money, my father had once called them. Ron had been into that for awhile, but luckily he outgrew it.

"So, where did you meet Gary?" I asked.

Zack replaced one wrench, reached for another, and scratched at the side of his face with a greasy finger.

"Penguin's. It's like this little neighborhood place where guys go to have a beer and watch the ball game. Gary was there all the time."

"The guys liked him, huh?"

"Oh, yeah. When Gary had money, he was your best friend. Not like a lotta guys. He'd buy rounds for the whole place."

"He do any betting?"

"Oh, hell, yes. Uh, pardon my French. Yeah, we all did. Bet on the playoffs, Superbowl, stuff like that."

"How about the horses?"

"That too. Gary'd take all our bets, then go to

the track. He sure loved that track. When we picked
a winner, he'd bring us our money."

"Minus his take."

"Well, yeah. Guy's not gonna spend that much
effort without making a little somethin'." He traded
wrenches again, then lifted some contraption out of
the engine.

"But nobody minded that."

"Why? Gary was always fair with us."

"Did you ever hear where the money came from
when he hit it big? Like the times he'd buy drinks
for everyone?"

"Naw, not really. Gary was a real smart guy.
Always had these big business deals going. He
prob'ly got these big commission checks all at once,
or somethin'."

Yeah, like the commission on a Rolex watch.

"Can you think of any reason somebody would
kill him?" I asked.

He raised up and looked straight at me for the
first time. His face was probably very good looking
under all the grease. He was about six feet tall, slim
build, with dark eyes and a nice smile.

"I sure can't," he said. "Down at Penguin's, anyway, he didn't have an enemy in the world."

I thanked him and left a business card in case
he thought of anything else. He stuck it into his shirt
pocket, where I imagined it staying right through
the wash cycle and coming out as a little white wad.

Two other visits yielded about the same infor-

mation. It was a bit early to catch the bartender at
Penguin's. Besides, I was getting tired. Talking to
people can really wear you down. I decided to head
for home in case Paul and his brood had returned
early. The drive across town gave me a chance to
think some more about Gary Detweiller. Who was
this, Robin Hood? Robbing from the rich to give to
the poor? If so, who would be mad enough to do him
in? Maybe tomorrow I'd head back to the rich side
of town.

As it turned out I didn't get a chance. I walked
in my front door to find Paul and Lorraine stretched
out on the couch with the TV blasting. Annie and
Joe sprinted through the living room just then chasing Rusty, who dashed for cover behind my legs as
soon as he saw me. I put my hands out to fend off
the attackers. Paul noticed me then and mouthed
some words in my direction. Lorraine mouthed
something at him, he nodded, then directed more
words at me. It felt like stepping into a Hitchcock
movie where the background music jangles so loudly
that the actual dialog is meaningless.

I told the kids Rusty needed to go out now —
alone. They set off toward the kitchen door. Making
my way over to the couch I picked up the remote
control and adjusted the television to a reasonable
level where human conversation could take place.

"How was your day?" I removed two empty
glasses from my Queen Anne coffee table and wiped
at wet rings with my sleeve.

"It was nice," Lorraine said. "We got a chance—" Joe plopped in her lap with enough force to knock the air out of her.

"Mom, when're we gonna eat?" he whined.

Lorraine turned to offer him some explanation, apparently forgetting that she'd been talking to me. Annie was tugging at Paul simultaneously, so I carried the dirty glasses and a crushed potato chip bag to the kitchen.

Yes, let's eat, I thought. I hated to do this to Pedro, but I had to get these guys out of my house.

"I'd rather go to McDonald's," Annie whined.

"But sweetheart, we can go to McDonald's at home. Pedro's is a place Daddy and Aunt Charlie and I really like." Lorraine's voice was kind and patient. Personally, I'd have told the kid to shut up and get in the car. Guess that's why I don't have kids.

"McDonald's." Annie kept her little voice firm, and Joe joined in. Soon it became a chant. Paul looked up at me helplessly. I shrugged. Anyone who's powerless at the mercy of a ten-year-old probably deserves it. We went to McDonald's.

Annie and Joe each ate about thirty cents worth of the burger from their kid meal boxes that I'd paid two dollars apiece for. The rest lay scattered over the table. They scampered off to the play yard where they crawled around through a series of hamster trails sized for kids.

Paul and Lorraine kept a conversation going of

sorts, interrupted by one or the other going to check on their offspring about every three minutes. I ate my Big Mac and fries and nodded at the right times, while my mind darted back and forth thinking about the people I'd talked to in the past few days. Who killed Gary Detweiller?

By three o'clock the next afternoon I was wondering who would kill Annie and Joe. I might be a good candidate. The sleeping bags were neatly rolled, the bags packed, and it was all I could do to resist carrying the stuff to the car myself. When the front doorbell rang I jumped.

"Anybody home?" Ron stuck his head in.

"Ron! You're back. Look who's here," I said taking him by the arm. Paul and Lorraine were in the kitchen. Annie and Joe stood off to the side eyeing Ron suspiciously. "Want to take the houseguests from hell back to your place for awhile?" I muttered under my breath.

"Not a bit," he smiled.

Paul had emerged from the kitchen just then. He and Ron clasped hands in a hearty shake. Lorraine got scooped up in one of Ron's giant hugs. I stood back and watched my brothers' contrasting interaction. Paul is tall and thin with dark hair and eyes, technically the better looking of the two. Ron is about five-ten and heftier. His dark hair is thin on top and shows touches of gray at the temples. Paul is the slacks and polo shirt type, while Ron chooses Levi's, western shirt, Stetson, and boots.

When he wants to look a little more dressed up, he'll add a bolo tie. Paul is quiet in a diffident sort of way, while Ron's softspoken manner suggests thoughtfulness. Not to say that we don't butt heads now and then. But I really am glad he's my partner.

I let Ron have the visitors all to himself for awhile. I offered drinks but no one was interested. I busied myself cleaning up the kitchen and gathering the guest towels and sheets into the washer. When Ron stood up to leave an hour later, the others did, too. It was a long drive back to Phoenix, they said.

I spent the rest of the evening gathering my sanity, cleaning up all traces of visitors, enjoying the peacefulness of my home without anyone else in it. Rusty lay sprawled out on his side near me, apparently exhausted. It wasn't until I was getting ready for bed that night that I remembered I hadn't even mentioned the case to Ron.

I dreamed that I was sitting in the living room holding a baby that was obviously mine. It screamed constantly despite everything I tried to calm it. Two other children, who looked suspiciously like Annie and Joe, romped through the house knocking over a porcelain figurine I'd had since I was a child. A nameless, faceless man in the picture was stretched out on the sofa, watching a ball game on TV and reaching occasionally for his beer can which left a huge wet ring on the coffee table. I awoke perspiring and breathing hard.

The bedside clock said it was almost six. No

point in trying to get back to sleep now. I put on a robe and slippers and went to the kitchen. The winter sky was faintly gray, the air cold. I started the coffee maker and let Rusty out to the back yard. By the time I'd gone to the bathroom and brushed my teeth, Rusty was waiting at the door, nose to the crack, shivering. The coffee was ready, so I poured a mug and curled up on the couch watching the morning news on TV while the hot liquid gradually woke me up.

By eight I had showered, dressed in gray wool slacks and a thick sweater, and was on my way to the office. I had to figure out a way to tell Ron that I'd taken a case in his absence and that I'd actually started to work on it. I didn't have long to plan my speech, either. He was already at his desk when I arrived.

"For who!" His brown eyes were incredulous.

"Whom, Ron."

He shot me a look. "You *know* what I mean. Why on earth would you want to get mixed up with Stacy North?"

"I didn't really want to," I tried to explain. "Well, she just looked so pitiful when she came in here that day. I thought I'd just be finding a stolen watch, which I did quite well, I believe."

"And now it's a murder case. You know I can't legally step into that," he reminded me.

"And you haven't," I reminded him. "I'm not the

investigator here. I'm just an interested party asking a few questions."

"Have you been representing this agency?"

I thought of the few business cards I'd handed
out. "I won't do it any more," I assured him.

"Charlie, Charlie." He took on that older-and-
wiser older brother look. "I know you can't seem to
resist somebody in trouble. You were always the kid
who picked up wounded birds, too. But nowadays
things are different. You can get yourself hurt,
maybe even killed, maybe even get this agency
sued." Now that really would be the worst.

"I get the feeling Stacy is afraid of Brad," I told
him. "You should have seen her when she thought
Brad was going to find out her watch was lost. Can
you imagine what he'd do if he found out about this
other man? Especially if Stacy is implicated in a
murder? Ron, I'm really afraid for her safety."

"What have you done so far?" he sighed.

I filled him in on the interviews with the family
and the list of names I'd found and so brilliantly
deciphered.

"You're withholding evidence." His voice was
flat, like nothing I did anymore would surprise him.

"Wait a minute! The wallet was on the victim
when the police found him. The list was in the
wallet. If they'd thought it important, they would
have taken it."

He pressed his lips together. He didn't agree

with my logic, I could tell, but he couldn't find a way
to argue with it either.

"I can't authorize you to work on this," he said.

"Will you do it then?"

"Charlie, I have umpteen million things waiting
here. The price of being gone a week."

"Then I'm going out to ask a few more unauthor-
ized questions."

"You wouldn't consider letting the police work
on their own case, I guess."

"Ron, I'm sure they're working on it, and I'm
sure they're doing a fine job." I walked out before
he could add anything.

Traffic on the freeway was heavy, moving at a
frustrating speed-up, slow-down pace. The sun had
topped Sandia Peak already, but thin streaky gray
clouds filtered out any warming effect. March is
such an ugly month. The charm of winter has long
since worn off, and the beauty of spring won't be
here for another six weeks or more. Spring winds
usually blow for most of March and April, leaving
spirits whipped and nerves raw. This is about the
only time of year I envy Paul and Lorraine's living
in Phoenix.

I took the San Mateo exit toward Academy Road
once again. This was beginning to feel like familiar
territory. Traffic all seemed to be heading the opposite direction, making me feel like the only person
in town who hadn't heard the air raid sirens. Low-
ering my sun visor against the glare, I continued my

easterly course. The same toothless guard from the other day protected the Tanoan gate and he waved me through like an old-timer.

Now that I was here, I couldn't decide whether to continue checking the names on my list or pay another visit to Stacy. The steady stream of outbound traffic warned me that I might not have much luck either way. Before I stirred up any more uninvolved parties it might be better to find out if there had been any new developments over the weekend. I pulled into Stacy's circular drive and rang her multi-chimed doorbell.

A dark shape wavered behind the beveled glass for a moment. The next thing I knew, I stood face-to-face with the man I'd once thought I would marry.

8

Brad North had put on a lot of weight. That was my first impression. He'd once been tall and thin. He still had the height, but everything had rounded out, giving him indistinct outlines. The soft jogging suit he wore accentuated the effect. His hair was still wavy brown, his eyes blue. At the moment his mouth hung slack. He was obviously dumbfounded to find me standing here.

"Hello, Brad."

His mouth worked a couple of times, settling finally into a tentative smile. "Charlie! What a surprise."

"Is Stacy home?" My mind groped for a reasonable explanation for my appearance.

Stacy showed up behind Brad's shoulder just then, questioning. When she saw me, her face went white.

"Stacy, now don't tell me you've forgotten that we'd planned to go out for breakfast." I noticed that she was still in her robe. "You did, didn't you?"

Luckily she picked up my cue. "Oh, Charlie, God, yes, I did forget." She glanced nervously at Brad, whose mouth had formed a straight line. "Brad, you remember my telling you that I ran into Charlie recently? I completely forgot that we were going out to breakfast today."

His eyes narrowed, but he didn't say anything.

"Can you give me a minute to get dressed?" she asked me. Turning to Brad again, she hesitantly met his stare. "Is it okay, Brad? I won't be gone long."

There was a moment's pause as Brad apparently wrestled between saying what he really felt and preserving his image before an outsider. "Sure. It's fine." Stacy dashed for the staircase.

I stood awkwardly on the porch, wondering just what was going on here. Did she really need permission to see an old friend?

"Well, come on in, Charlie. We're letting all the cold air in." Brad closed the door behind me. "Let me show you around while Stacy gets dressed."

I had no idea how much Stacy'd told him, but didn't think it would be wise to admit I'd already had the grand tour. His version was a bit different from Stacy's anyway. He took particular pride in pointing out the art objects and paintings. With each came an explanation of where it had come from and either a) how much it cost, or b) how much it was worth, or c) what a fantastic deal he'd negotiated in buying it. I began keeping a surreptitious count on my fingers and was amazed to find by the end of the tour that Brad had supposedly visited forty-three different countries. Either that or he was a tremendous bullshitter.

Stacy found us in the study, where Brad was going into an explanation of each of the famous person photos, making sure I was fully informed about how well he knew each of them. I looked in her direction and faked a tiny yawn. She almost smiled.

"Well, Brad, it's been just fascinating," I interrupted. "We'll be going now. You must be totally exhausted after taking me through all your travels."

He trailed us to the front door, missing my sarcasm as he raved about the wonderful brunch at the club. We really should try it. We couldn't go wrong if we had the Eggs Benedict. I ignored this blatant fishing for an invitation and waved an impersonal little salute his direction as Stacy and I got into my Jeep.

Stacy was quiet in the car and I had to restrain myself from asking whether Brad was always such a braggart, or if that little show was entirely for my benefit. After all, look at everything I'd missed out on.

"I'm glad you picked up on my clue about breakfast back there," I commented.

She smiled tightly. "Charlie, this is very risky. Why did you show up unannounced?"

"Because taking people off guard is usually the best way to get straight answers." Geez, what was the big deal? "Okay, sorry. I hope this doesn't cause any trouble at home. I honestly thought Brad would have left for work by now."

"He's going over some papers at home this morning," she said sullenly.

"Obviously. Look, I was just going to ask a quick question or two. I didn't mean to take up much time. The breakfast thing was the only idea I could come up with on such short notice. We can skip it if you want."

"Oh, no. I mean, that would just take more explanations. Let's find someplace to eat. It'll be okay as long as I'm not gone too long."

I wanted to point out to her that she was a grown woman, allowed to eat out with a friend without offering a dissertation on her reasons why. But I let it drop. I pulled into the parking lot of a coffee shop I'd seen on the way up.

"Is this okay?"

She must have caught the edge in my voice because she smiled and relaxed for the first time.

"It's fine, Charlie. And thanks." She squeezed my hand. "I did need to get out of the house."

I let that pass, too.

We were seated right away and decided to treat ourselves to huevos rancheros, juice, and coffee, and to top it off with a danish. The important stuff out of the way, I got down to the questions.

"No, I haven't heard a word from the police," she replied. "I'm a nervous wreck every time the doorbell rings. Brad has hung around the house like a watchdog. I can tell he's suspicious."

No wonder. She was as jumpy as an escaped convict.

"There was a small article about Gary in the newspaper, but I never got a chance to read it. I was afraid Brad would catch me and wonder why I was following the case."

"Stacy, he doesn't actually read over your shoulder, does he? How would he know what you're reading?" It was like talking to a five-year-old.

"I know." She sighed and drummed her fingers nervously on the table until our food arrived.

I gave myself over to the pleasure of eating. The combination of flavors — tortilla, eggs, beans, cheese, and green chile — filled me with satisfaction. Stacy picked at hers, taking a tiny forkful at a time. She'd lost weight in the last week.

"Stace, you gotta eat," I reminded her gently. "Worrying about this isn't going to change anything. Look at it this way, if the police haven't made the connection yet, chances are they won't. Gary Det-weiller had a lot of people in his life, a lot of them with stronger reasons to hate him than you did."

She perked up. "You have an idea who did it?" she asked eagerly.

"Well, no. But I'll keep working on it. Promise. And you can help me. Just keep trying to think of anything Detweiller might have said to you, even in the most casual way. Anyone who might have been angry with him, anyone he might have shafted."

"I've been trying," she assured me, "but nothing comes to mind. It's just so hard, trying to act normal around Brad, while this thing is weighing on me."

She fidgeted with her food some more. She wouldn't be any help on the case, I could see that now. I'd have to think of some other avenues. When I dropped her off at home a little while later, Brad met her at the door. I waved from the car and drove off. We'd been gone exactly an hour.

Three blocks away, on another of Tanoan's winding little side streets, I found Ben Reed at home. He, too, wore a jogging suit and top-brand running shoes. His once-red hair was interspersed with so much gray that it appeared pale apricot. His face and hands were covered with freckles. He greeted me with an easy smile, but didn't invite me in.

"Gary Detweiller? Name doesn't ring a bell," he said. He took the fuzzy newspaper photo from me and stared at it. "The face I do know." He handed the photo back. "Guy hung around the club, sucking up to the members. I knew from the first time I saw him that he didn't belong. But he managed to get invited somehow. I don't even know who he came with. I saw him around, oh, probably a half-dozen times."

"Did you ever speak to him?"

"Let's say *he* spoke to me. Tried to hit me up to finance some business deal he was getting into."

"What did you tell him?"

"Not only no, but hell, no," he chuckled.

"Did you know he had your name and phone number on a coded list in his wallet?"

Reed looked puzzled. "Why would he? We never did any business."

"Maybe it was his prospect list."

"That's kind of spooky," he said. "Like he watched us all, and targeted those he thought he could work on."

"What about the women? Did you notice him targeting them?"

He thought about it for a minute. "Now that you mention it, I did. He was a good-looking guy, you know. I don't think he had to try too hard with the women. I noticed some flirting going on at a couple of the Friday night dinner dances."

"Anyone in particular?"

"Nah, he seemed to spread the charm pretty equally everywhere."

I hoped that was the impression everyone else

got, too. I thanked Ben Reed for his information and left. It was nearing noon, but I wasn't the least bit hungry after the huge breakfast with Stacy. I headed back to the office.

Sally met me in the kitchen to let me know that Ron would be at the county courthouse all afternoon. She would be leaving at one, and the phones had really been busy all morning with people trying to reach Ron after his week-long absence. Would I be around to take the calls?

I said I would, although I couldn't see that it made much difference whether they left a message with me or on the answering machine. She then proceeded to hand me a list of Ron's replies. Tell this one such and such. Tell that one something else. Apparently he had anticipated the deluge of calls, and planned well for it. Why hadn't he put off his day at the courthouse until tomorrow?

Sally must have heard these thoughts run through my head because she looked at me sympathetically.

"Do you want some lunch before I go?" she asked.

I explained why I didn't and we spent the next thirty minutes going over some pending correspondence. By the time she left, my head was full of other things and it took me awhile to get back on track with the Detweiller case.

My yellow sheet of names and addresses was pretty rumpled by now, but I smoothed it out and looked at it. I'd checked off around half the names without making any serious inroads with anybody. I stared at them, trying to find a common thread, some pattern to the odd mix. I jotted a few notes from each of the conversations, hoping a killer's name would jump out at me. Again, the obvious differences I'd noticed before. The group was pretty evenly divided between the haves and the have-nots. Neither group had been particularly informative. Maybe I'd try backtracking to each group's common ground, their hangouts.

That decided, I spent the rest of the afternoon catching up on my own work. Ron had left a crumpled pile of travel expenses in the middle of my desk. I organized them by category and filed them where I could find them again when the credit card bills arrived. Accounting tends to pile up when I'm not looking. One week everything is done. The next week, a new month has begun and suddenly I'm behind again.

I usually bill clients on the first and fifteenth, so I was already several days behind on that. Fortunately, since Ron was out of town there weren't a lot of new entries in his log book. That part of it only took an hour or so. I posted the billing into the computer, reviewed the past due accounts, and printed statements. Very few of our cases are as clandestine as Stacy's with the client paying in cash. Most of the work is done for law firms or insurance companies. Those people like everything in writing and neatly organized. Ron isn't the most organized person in the world so that's where I come in.

By four o'clock I had a neat stack of envelopes on my desk ready to drop in the nearest mailbox. Tomorrow I could post the expenses and run some preliminary month-end figures. Then I'd have the tax returns to work on. I'd almost forgotten them. Normally I'd have done them by mid-February, but my computer had been in for repairs for two weeks, which had really thrown a kink in things. Another reason I should have sent Stacy away when she first showed up.

Rusty rode with me this time. First stop, Tanoan Country Club. I hoped to arrive before the dinner crowd, perhaps while the wait staff was setting up. For once, I got my wish. The maitre d' I'd seen in action the other day was bustling around, sans jacket and accent, barking orders at the waiters. I hung to the side, not particularly wanting to attract his attention. He wasn't the sort to talk about the clientele. No, I wanted somebody with either vengeance or gossip on his mind. Within three or four minutes the maitre d' had been called into the kitchen on some emergency, and I spotted my chance. A young waitress (probably called a server here) was laying out place settings on a table for eight near me. She looked about twenty. Her blond hair was pulled into a pony tail at the very top of her head, where it spewed forth like a waterspout. Her head bobbed up and down in time with some internal tune she hummed between chomps on a huge wad of bubblegum.

"Excuse me," I whispered. "Could you come here a minute?"

She glanced around to see who might be watching. The boss safely out of sight, she sidestepped toward me.

"Do you work here on Friday nights?"

She nodded, the gum popping again.

"Could I ask you a few questions, privately?"

She checked out the room again, hesitating. The other waitpersons seemed oblivious, each wrapped up in their own tasks. The boss had not reappeared yet. Still, she seemed nervous. I dug into the side pocket of my purse and came up with a ten dollar bill. At the same time, I indicated a small alcove off the entry. It was out of sight of the dining room.

"Okay," she agreed, "just a couple of minutes though. Andre gets really ticked off if he catches us goofing around."

I produced the photo of Gary Detweiller. "Do you remember seeing this man at the Friday dinner dances a few times?"

"Oh, yeah. For an old guy, he was real sexy. He had this smile. . . you know. Well, I don't know how to explain it, but it kinda made your heart go faster when he turned this smile on you."

"Did he flirt a lot? Like with all the girls here?"

"Look, you're not his wife are you?" She eyed me suspiciously.

"Not hardly. Just tell me about him."

"He mostly flirted with the club members. I mean, he'd flash that smile at us girls when he placed his order or like when he wanted another drink. But he really poured it on with the rich women. And sometimes when their husbands were sitting right there."

"Anyone in particular?"

She glanced upward, thinking. "Not really. Just about everyone. There was this one blond lady. She always wore a black fur coat. Her husband's a big chubby guy who's always obnoxious to the help. They're in here all the time but I'm not sure what her name is. Want me to find out?"

"No, no. It's not that important." Great. All I needed was for this chick to make the connection between Detweiller and Stacy. "Any others?"

"A few, but I don't know their names either. Oh, Ms. Delvecchio. I think he put the moves on her once. I'd gone into the bar," she nodded toward a doorway behind us, "and was coming back with a trayful of drinks. He had whispered something to her, and she laughed about it. Then she, you know, kind of like blushed." She raised her eyes upward again, thinking. "I can't really remember any others."

"Well, thanks, you've been helpful. Look, don't mention this to anyone, okay." I nodded toward the ten dollar bill in her hand. "It's just between us."

She peered cautiously through a potted palm

before stepping back into the dining room. I didn't have much hope that she'd really keep our conversation secret, but she didn't know my name so how far could they trace me?

Downstairs, the offices beside the main entrance were quiet, although a few lights remained on. Spotting a computer monitor that was still on, I had a flash of inspiration. It took me about two minutes to figure out the menus and find Carla Delvecchio's address in the membership roster. I memorized it quickly, just before I looked up to find a secretary approaching. She was glaring right at me.

9

"Who *are* you?" The secretary stood directly in front of the desk with arms folded. If her blue power suit and short masculine hairstyle were designed to intimidate, they sure worked.

"This computer isn't down," I said, clicking the few necessary keys to sign off.

"Excuse me?"

"You didn't place a service call to IBM?" I stood, gathering my coat around me, slinging my purse's shoulder strap into place.

"No, we did not." Her voice was pointed, and not the least bit friendly.

"Well, then someone gave me wrong information," I said, pretending to consult some paperwork in my purse. "Sorry to have troubled you." I headed for the door.

"Wait, let me see that work order," she said.

I pretended not to hear her. My feet didn't slow down until I reached my car. My heart didn't slow down until I was six blocks away.

The sun was low over the volcanoes by now. There wouldn't be a fabulous sunset tonight though. This morning's thin clouds had spread and the wind picked up. Tumbleweeds skipped across the road, lodging against the white block Tanoan wall on my right. I took Wyoming south to Lomas. The worst of the go-home traffic had dissipated, but it still took nearly twenty-five minutes to find Penguin's bar.

It was one of those small neighborhood places, the kind with its own set of regulars who probably come by for a beer every night of the week and stay late on Mondays for football. The kind where a strange face sticks out like a bum at the country club. I figured this out when no fewer than fourteen heads turned to stare as I walked in the door. Ninety percent of the crowd was male. In my wool slacks and sweater that had seemed casual at Tanoan, I suddenly felt overdressed here.

Penguin's was one room, squarish. A third of the space at the far end was filled by two pool tables. A lamp hung over each, a poor plastic imitation of stained glass. Both tables were in use, encircled by men in work clothes with patches over the breast pocket disclosing their names. The bar was directly in front of me, with the intervening space filled by a dozen or so square formica topped tables flanked by four chairs each.

Few tables were occupied, but the bar was crowded. Since I wanted to talk to the bartender, I squeezed through to the one empty stool.

"Yes, ma'am?" The bartender was forty-something, medium height, skinny, with a dark hairline that had receded in a large inverted W. His sharp facial features were softened by age. There was a tiredness around eyes that had seen too much, jowls that sagged from a lack of smiling.

"I'll have a white w....," I glanced down the bar at the other patron's drinks. "Make that a Bud Light."

He shoved a large mug under the tap without a word. Meanwhile, I felt other eyes upon me, and looked up at the man beside me, a big guy in his mid-fifties wearing a blue work shirt and pants. He turned to stare into his beer when I sent a little smile his way. I planned to sip my beer slowly and hoped the crowd would clear out a little so I could speak to the bartender without twenty other sets of ears picking up the whole thing. Since I'm not a beer drinker, this should not prove difficult.

Other conversations began to pick up again. The TV set in the corner carried the news and I remembered that football season was over. Within twenty minutes, several of the men at the bar left. I took another sip and bided my time. By seven o'clock there were only five or six people scattered around the room. The man next to me hadn't budged.

"Shame about Gary Detweiller," I commented after trying out some standard small-talk.

He sipped. "Yup. You knew Gary?"

"Friend of a friend," I said. "She's pretty broken up about it."

"Lady friend, huh? Well, tell her not to get too broke up. He had a bunch of 'em. And a wife."

"No kidding!" I feigned surprise as well as I could. "Well, Linda always did know how to pick 'em." I took another sip. The bartender had walked over to check our drinks, which were still going fine. He wiped the bar, casually joining the conversation.

"I heard Gary had a lot of friends, though," I said to either of them.

"Oh, yeah, Gary was a good ol' boy," my drinking buddy said. "He was sure in here every night, wasn't he, Pete?"

"Yeah, he sure was." Pete's voice sounded tired, his enthusiasm underwhelming.

"I heard he carried a fair amount of action, too. Bets, I mean," I hinted.

"Lotta guys in here sent their bets with Gary. He sure loved those race tracks. When it wasn't racing season, he'd bet on the games."

"Everybody like him pretty well?"

"I'd say so, wouldn't you, Pete? I don't know nobody didn't like Gary. Why, he'd come in here sometimes after he'd won big, and buy drinks for everybody. Ain't that right, Pete?"

Pete finally cracked a smile. He should have done it more often, he had nice teeth. "Yeah, that was always fun," he said. "The guys'd get real excited. And he was a real good tipper, too."

My buddy had finished his third beer by then. He slapped some money down on the bar. "Gotta get on home. See ya later, Pete." He walked toward the back of the room, acknowledging two men at a table along the way. He stopped at a pay phone set into a small alcove at the back.

I glanced around the room. It looked like the early crowd had all gone and a few new ones now filled in. It was a slack time, before the late crowd came, and Pete stood around, not particularly busy. I was the only one left in this section of the bar.

"Pete, who might have wanted Gary Detweiller dead?" I asked.

"Why you asking so many questions? You're not this nosy because some friend of yours had the hots for Gary, are you?"

"I work for a private investigation agency. One of our clients is concerned about being implicated. I'd like to find out who really did it."

"Shoot, I don't know," he said. He'd relaxed with me now, and I felt he was being truthful. "You heard Willie. Most everybody here liked the guy."

"He had a lot of women though. You think one of them might have been mad at him? Maybe he promised somebody more than he planned to deliver."

"Maybe so. Look, I don't get a lot of last names here. Debbie, Linda, Susan — that tell you anything? Gary usually had somebody different with him every week or so. And they weren't teenagers. They knew the score. Gary took 'em out, spent money on 'em. Past that, I don't think they expected a lot from him."

"What about the gambling? Anybody ever lose big? Anybody with a grudge there?"

"Who knows? Maybe. But around here we never heard about it. Gary had this image, you know. Like he always had to be friendly and happy. Everybody's pal, he was."

Why was this so difficult? Wasn't there anybody out there who would admit that they hated Gary Detweiller? I left Pete a generous tip and a business card, asking him to let me know if he thought of anything else.

It was pitch dark out by now and the wind had picked up to a bitter whine. Sand from a neighboring vacant lot whipped through the paved parking lot, leaving little drifts against the concrete parking bumpers. I pulled my coat closer around me and fished in my pocket for the keys. Then I noticed that my Jeep was sitting crippled by a flat front tire. Shit.

I learned to change a tire once. It was in driver education, and I didn't actually do it, we just had to sit through a film on the procedure. I could probably

manage if I had to, but I didn't really want to. My
head was a little stuffy from drinking the beer, and
I really wasn't dressed for getting down on my hands
and knees. Rusty sat up in the back seat, his ears
cocked toward me. Glancing around the parking lot
I considered my options. I could go inside and ask
for volunteers. But I didn't really want to do that.
You never know what kind of payment men in bars
expect for their good deeds. I could use the phone
inside and call Ron. Unfortunately, I wasn't ready
for the lecture I knew I'd get. Already, he didn't want
me on this case. And there was no way he'd believe
I'd just stopped in this cozy little spot for a brewsky
after work. Not my style.

Penguin's sat on a small side street, two lots
away from Lomas Boulevard, a major street. I
walked up to the corner to check out further options.
Why had I let my AAA membership expire? About
three blocks west I could see the lighted sign of a
tire company. I might be in luck after all.

The wind tore through my slacks, sending cold
all the way up my legs, as I fought it for the three
blocks. The windows were all dark and an employee
in dark coveralls was locking the door as I approached.

"Sorry, we're closed ma'am," he said as soon as
he saw me. He was about my age, with blond hair
that separated into greasy tendrils and hands per-
manently blackened from handling tires. A patch
above his pocket said his name was Bob.

"Please, I'm really in a bind." I hated sounding like a helpless female. I explained about the flat and told him I wouldn't need it repaired until tomorrow. Tonight I just needed the spare put on.

"The service truck's locked inside," he pointed out.

"I have the jack and the spare," I said. "I'll pay extra."

Those must have been the three magic words, although Bob wasn't exactly gracious in accepting my offer.

"Where's the vehicle?" he asked grudgingly.

"Penguin's parking lot. You know where that is?"

We'd walked across the tire store's parking area during the conversation, and he unlocked the doors of a seventy-three Mustang. Cherry red, restored to perfection, it was obviously his pride and joy. "Hop in," he said.

Fifteen minutes later my flat tire lay in the trunk of his car, and my Jeep was ready to go again. Bob told me to come by the tire store sometime after ten in the morning and he'd have the tire repaired. He said he didn't want to take payment for the tire change, that he'd been on his way to Penguin's anyway. I gave him a twenty and said I'd feel better if he took it.

Rusty was practically pawing at the windows by this time, worried about me and eager to get out of confinement. Probably hungry, too. I know I was

starving. We turned west on Lomas with only one
stop on the way home — Mac's Steak in the Rough,
where I treated us both to a high-fat dinner of fried
steak strips. We munched them in the car and felt
much better when we got home.

I couldn't wait to get out of the wool I'd worn all
day, and Rusty couldn't wait to use the backyard.
We each rushed to our respective needs. I slipped on
soft sweats, glad to be rid of the itchy wool waistband around my middle. I heated water for tea and
peeked out the back window to check on Rusty. He
was busy rolling on his back in the dead winter
grass, rubbing his nose almost sensuously against
its earthy smell. I noticed one small light on in Elsa
Higgins's kitchen. It had been several days since I'd
spoken to her. Tomorrow I'd better give her a call.

Taking my cup of tea to the living room, I
switched on some soft music and pulled out my
notebook. I made a few notes about the conversations I'd had today before I found myself nodding off.
Not even ten o'clock and I was beat.

The price of going to bed early is waking up
early. By six o'clock my eyes were staring fixedly at
the ceiling. By seven thirty I was at my desk, up to
my elbows in tax returns. When Sally paged me on
the intercom to tell me that Bob from Black's Tire
Store was on the line, I nearly jumped. When had
Sally come in? I was amazed to look at my watch
and find that it was nearly noon.

"Ms. Parker? This is Bob, from last night? Afraid I got some bad news for you about your tire."

"What's the matter, Bob?"

"I don't know if you realized this or not, but that tire wasn't just punctured, it was slashed. We can't fix it. You're gonna need a new one."

"Slashed?" It took a minute for his words to register. "You mean someone did it deliberately?"

"Yes, ma'am. It's a big cut, at least four inches long."

My mind raced back to the previous evening. Had this been random vandalism or had someone targeted me? I thought I'd stayed pretty low-key, talking only to Pete the bartender and that other man who sat beside me. I know Pete couldn't have done it, he'd been in sight all evening. But the other man? He sure didn't look the type. And he'd been friendly enough. What about the other patrons, though? Few faces stuck in my memory — they'd come and gone all evening. I hadn't particularly watched any of them. But obviously one of them had watched me, probably listening in on my conversation at the bar.

I told Bob to go ahead and mount a new tire on my wheel and I'd come by this afternoon to pick it up.

Ron was gone at the moment; besides, I really didn't want to tell him about this yet. After swearing Sally to secrecy I told her about the whole evening.

She didn't give it much importance. "Maybe it was just plain vandalism," she suggested.

That answer didn't satisfy me. I stomped rather grumpily into the kitchen to refill my coffee mug, then went back to my tax returns. By two o'clock my head was spinning with numbers and I was ready for a break from the tedium. Rusty and I decided to quit for the day. We headed uptown toward Black's Tire. Bob showed me the old tire with the clean cut in the sidewall. I waited in their customer lounge while he replaced the spare with the new tire on the car and flinched as I paid the bill. It had turned out to be a very expensive beer last night.

Thinking back over the notes I'd made last night, something came to mind. I decided to pay another call on the Detweillers. Maybe I could catch Jean before she left for work.

Last night's wind had howled all night, but it left a beautiful day in its wake. The brown cloud of pollution which sits over the city for months at a time, held in place by a winter inversion, had blown away, leaving a clear blue sky that almost dazzled the eyes. The sun came through, deceptively warm. Growing up here I've seen sixty degree days in January and twenty degree days in March. Winter's not over til it's over. But that doesn't stop me from enjoying the pretty days when they happen.

Apparently Jean Detweiller felt the same. I found her on the front porch, attacking the door with sandpaper. She wore jeans and a faded sweatshirt with the sleeves pushed up. Her hair was held back by a red kerchief.

"Hi, Charlie." She was breathing hard from exertion. "I've decided I can't stand this place any more. I've gotta clean it up or burn it down."

"Spring fever, maybe," I suggested.

"Maybe so."

I noticed the drapes were open today and the windows had been freshly washed. Leaves and debris had been raked from the rock landscaping around the shrubs.

"You really have been working at it," I commented.

"I need to stay busy," she replied. She resumed sanding at the flaky paint.

"This has to be hard on you," I told her.

She paused a moment and straightened up, fixing me with an even gaze. "You know, I don't know if I ought to say this but losing Gary was probably the best thing that ever happened to me."

"What do you mean?" I asked, faintly startled that she'd voice her feelings to me.

"You know how some people act one way around others and completely different at home?"

Most people do, I thought.

"You know, around his friends Gary was Mr. Generous, the good guy who said what they wanted to hear, gave 'em what they wanted. Gary was a dreamer. He made people believe that he really could make those dreams come true. I guess that's

how I got attracted in the first place. But later, it—
well, it wasn't really like that." She suddenly got
busy working on one particular spot.

"What do you mean?" I prompted. I thought of
Josh's comments about his father chasing after gold
mines.

She sanded more furiously. I waited.

"I don't know," she hedged, not wanting to say.
"It's just that, you know, I got so tired of scrounging
by on my measly paycheck. Life was always such a
struggle, trying to afford things for Josh, trying to
pay the bills and keep the house up. And then Gary
would get his hands on some money, and instead of
helping with the bills, I'd find out he bought drinks
for everyone down at Penguin's."

I waited, letting her get the feelings out.

"Or worse, I'd find out that a *business trip* he
said he took was really an excuse to sneak off with
some woman and spend a weekend at the race
track." She dropped her sandpaper onto a heap of
crumpled pieces and picked up a fresh one.

"I put up with that shit for years, Charlie. For
Josh's sake I probably would have put up with it
still. But truthfully, I'm just as glad it worked out
this way."

"How's Josh doing, by the way?"

"Okay. He'll get over it."

"They were close?"

She didn't answer right away. When she did, her
tone was cynical. "They were alike," was all she said.

"Is Josh home now?" I asked. "I thought I'd try to talk to him again, too."

"He's not home from school yet," she said. "Today's my day off, so I doubt he'll be back anytime soon. He's going through this independent stage, wants to be off on his own. Spending time with Mom wouldn't be cool."

"Has Josh ever been in trouble? Drugs, gangs, any of that?"

"Not gangs. It'd be too hard for him to hide that. Drugs? Who knows? I've never found the stuff, but then I don't go into his room. Josh and his friends seem to be more into rock music and noisy cars."

And probably girls. Given Josh's stunning looks, I'd be willing to bet he had girls trailing him everywhere. Maybe that's what Jean meant when she said Josh and Gary were alike. I thanked Jean for her time and wished her well with her fix-up projects.

It was nearly six o'clock now, and I realized my chances of finding Josh hanging around school were probably worse than zero. I assumed he went to Highland High, it was the closest to their home, although I should have asked Jean.

The sun had ducked below the horizon minutes before, giving the city a curious pink-gold glow. This might have been what Coronado and his men sought when they heard rumors of the seven golden cities of Cibola. Not gold at all, but the appearance of it. Without much hope, I cruised by the high school anyway. Its adobe colored stucco walls stood silent and golden in the fading light. The parking lot was completely empty. A couple of nearby hangouts were similarly deserted. I yawned. It had been a long day.

Rusty lay stretched out on the back seat, so I figured out what he would vote to do. We headed home. I spent the evening going over my notes again. The facts just weren't telling me much, and I didn't yet know enough about the personalities to know what emotions lay under the surface. I went to bed frustrated.

10

Tuesday morning I awoke early with Josh Detweiller on my mind. Maybe I could catch him before class. I dressed quickly in jeans, t-shirt, and tennies, then added a denim jacket which I hoped would be warm enough. I had neither the time nor inclination to do much with my hair, so I pulled it up into a pony tail. It was seven thirty when I pulled into the student parking lot at Highland High. A few cars dotted the lot. I was early enough to watch most of them arrive.

I parked in a spot at the far edge of the lot, near the gate. This should give me a clear view of the incoming traffic, which seemed headed toward the parking spaces nearest the buildings. Josh's car wasn't difficult to spot with its primer gray body and blackened windows. I started my engine when I saw him approach and followed him to his parking place. He didn't seem to notice me pulling in beside him.

"Hey, Josh, remember me?" I called out to him as he stepped from his car.

He gave me a blank look.

"Charlie Parker. I came by your house the other day."

His mind struggled to figure out who I was and what I was doing here. I used the time to circle the front of my car and join him. We fell into step walking across the parking lot.

"I was asking about your dad the other day," I reminded. "How are things going now?"

Recognition finally dawned, but he acted like he'd remembered me all along. "Fine."

"Fine? Just — fine."

"Yeah, just — fine."

"Have you heard any more about who might have done it? Have the police been around again?"

"I don't think so. I haven't been home much."

"How's your mom doing?"

"Okay, I guess. We don't see each other much." His tone was neutral, not revealing whether this was his idea or hers.

"I visited Larry Burke the other day," I told him. "From what he told me, he must have been the last one to see your dad alive. Except for the killer."

We followed a series of sidewalks between buildings. I followed Josh's lead, turning when he did.

"Do you think there's any chance Larry might have killed your father?" I asked. "He could be lying about the sequence of events that night. Maybe your dad didn't really take him home first. Maybe they went to your house, Larry shot him, then walked home."

Josh shrugged. "How would I know?"

We walked quietly for a few minutes. What motive would Larry Burke have, anyway, I reasoned, now that I'd brought up the question. Apparently Gary Detweiller shared the wealth, so why would Larry kill him? Unless they'd had some argument over a woman, or money?

"Have you had any other ideas about it since we talked the last time?" I asked Josh.

"Not really." We stood now in the doorway to a classroom. "Look, the bell's gonna ring in just a minute." He nodded toward the room, looking for a way out of the conversation.

"Yeah, okay. I gotta go anyway. Could we meet after school some day for a Coke?"

The request took him by surprise. "Sure, I guess. We usually hang out at Video Madness."

"Okay, maybe tomorrow." I watched him walk into the classroom, where he slapped hands with a couple of other guys in a teen male greeting ritual.

A bell jangled with loud heart-stopping ferocity, effectively silencing all other sound. Walking back to the parking lot, I thought back to my own school days, before gangs, blatant drug use, and almost obligatory teen sex. Although I'd been a teen in the seventies, those things were still not the norm for my generation. Life had been much easier then.

Not knowing any other way to avoid getting back to work on my tax returns, it looked like I had no other choice but to go to the office. There were still a couple of people I'd like to talk to in the Detweiller case, but they could wait. Plus, I'd really like to know how the police investigation was coming along, but didn't think I'd get a lot of information from Kent Taylor in homicide. Maybe I could hit Ron up to talk to him.

"Wow, you look like something fresh from high school," Sally commented when I walked into the kitchen.

"I am. Just got back from talking to Josh Detweiller."

"Are you still on that tangent?" Ron asked, coming into the room.

I poured myself a mug of coffee and offered him some. He let me fill his mug, too, and proceeded to add three spoons of sugar.

"I'm learning quite a lot about the victim," I told him. "But I still haven't found anyone who seems to have hated the man. Why would someone want to kill a guy that nobody disliked?"

He chuckled. "If it were that easy, don't you think the police would already have the answer? Charlie, did it ever occur to you that someone you've talked to is lying? I mean, people aren't always straight with us."

I resisted the urge to pop him one. Of course I wasn't naive enough to think that everyone was going to tell the truth. But, in fact, isn't that what I'd been doing? Taking all my suspects at face value? I returned thoughtfully to my desk.

The rest of the morning seemed to fly. Getting into tax returns is an all-consuming task, with one schedule leading to the next form, leading to the next worksheet. I had preliminary numbers penciled in before I realized a fundamental mistake in my depreciation schedules. I'd have to go back to the computer and do a couple of adjusting entries before I would have any real figures to go by.

Sally stopped in to ask whether I'd want lunch. I couldn't believe it, but it was already twelve-thirty. I asked if she'd mind getting me a sandwich. Sometime later she appeared with turkey on whole wheat, which I held in my left hand while my right hand skipped over the keys on my calculator. I took bites between calculating and penciling in new numbers.

Sally left for the day, and Ron seemed intent on his own work. He'd been on the phone most of the morning, making routine calls on a skip trace. I switched on the answering machine after the phone interrupted me for the second time in fifteen minutes. Tax returns are something I don't do well with interruptions.

"Why don't we take a dinner break?" Ron's voice startled me, so intent had I been on Form 4562.

I glanced at my watch. It was already six o'clock. I set my pencil down and rubbed at my burning eyes. Most of the schedules were done, and hopefully correct. It was time to let them rest a few days, then I'd review them to see if any mistakes stuck out.

"Pedro's?" I asked.

"Where else?" He crossed the room and closed the blinds for me. "I've already checked the front door, returned all the calls that came in on the machine, and turned out the lights everywhere but here," he said.

"Wow, you must be hungry. One car or two?" I asked.

"Two. We're probably both gonna want to go straight home afterward."

Pedro's is a tiny Mexican restaurant, just six blocks from my house. It's a couple of streets off the main plaza in Old Town, so most of the tourists miss it. We've been coming here since we were children, and Pedro and his wife Concha have practically adopted us. Tonight, there were two other vehicles out front when we pulled up.

One was a dusty pickup truck of indeterminate color belonging to another regular, Manny. The other was local but I didn't recognize it. Rusty began to get excited as soon as he saw where we were. Pawing at the side window, he whimpered impatiently.

"Hold on, hold on," I told him. "We'll be there in a minute."

Pedro relaxes the city health code regularly for us, keeping a corner table for us where Rusty can lie in the shadows, keeping watch for fallen tortilla chips. None of the other regulars seem to mind, but I usually take the precaution of checking the room first before letting Rusty in.

It's a small place, with a long handcarved bar from Mexico dominating the entire back wall. Six tables fill the tiny room to capacity. Manny sat at his usual table in the far right corner. His clothes were as dusty as his truck, nothing unusual, and he sat with his back to the wall as he watched the room and silently tossed back tequila shooters. I've seen him do five or six during the time it takes me to eat a meal, and he'll still be going at them when I leave. Pedro says Manny has the insides of a teenager.

Another table, this one on the right hand side of the room near the windows, was occupied by a couple who seemed far more wrapped up in each other than anything else. Otherwise, the place was empty. Pedro stood behind the bar. He caught my eye and nodded. Rusty was overjoyed when I let him out of the Jeep.

The three of us took our usual table in the front left corner. By the time we were seated Pedro had appeared with a basket of chips, a small bowl of salsa, and two foamy margaritas. Just the right amount of salt on the rim, the right amount of tangy lime, the drink was what I needed at the moment to unknot my cramped neck muscles. We munched on the chips while he delivered a check to the couple's table. Manny raised his grizzled gray and black whiskered chin to us, the only show of recognition we ever get from him.

"Here you go, move those glasses please," Concha bustled toward us carrying two plates so hot she had to carry them with potholders. Pedro had apparently signalled our usual order to her even before we were seated.

The smells of meat, cheese, and chile assailed the senses, making me eager to dig right in. Concha patted me on the shoulder as she walked away, leaving us to do just that. I tossed Rusty an extra tortilla chip to pacify him while I cut into my chicken enchiladas, smothered in green chile and sour cream. It was a good ten minutes before either Ron or I stopped to say a word.

"How was everything?" Concha came back to check on us, wiping her hands on her apron. She and Pedro are almost like Latino caricatures of the old Jack Sprat nursery rhyme. She is short and round, obviously having sampled much of her own cooking. Pedro is not much taller than his wife but skinny as a pole, probably attributable to his constantly being in motion. He flits around like a hummingbird, serving drinks, rinsing glasses, wiping the tables and the bar. You rarely see him sit.

"Umm, wonderful as always," I assured Concha.

"Good. You finish now, we'll visit later." She waddled back toward the kitchen. She and Pedro live here, too, in a small apartment they've made for themselves at the back.

"So, how's the case coming?" Ron asked, wiping red chile from the corners of his mouth.

"I feel kind of stumped," I admitted. "I've talked to so many people, but I just don't feel like I'm getting any answers."

"Remember — motive, means, and opportunity," he reminded. "Listen to what people tell you, but read between the lines. Listen to your gut instincts about people."

"I think I've found several who might have had motive. Maybe I just need to ask more questions to find out about the other two factors."

"The rest of this week looks pretty loaded for me," he said, "but maybe by the first of next week I can free up some time to help you."

"Thanks, but don't worry about it just yet. I'd like to work on it a little longer myself."

"Just remember, there is still an active police investigation going on here," he said. "If you uncover any evidence at all, you better turn it in or you're looking at trouble."

I shot him a look. I'm not that stupid, Ron. "Oh, that reminds me, do you think you could get any information out of Kent Taylor? I'd love to know what angles they're working on."

He chuckled. "I seriously doubt it, Charlie. What

do you think? I just walk in there and request a copy of the file, and I get it? Not hardly."

"Okay, okay. Be patient with me. I'm just learning how these things work." Maybe I *am* that stupid.

He didn't mention it. We finished our drinks and visited a couple of minutes with Pedro and Concha before saying goodnight. I started home but found I really wasn't in the mood for a quiet evening in front of the TV. The case still nagged at me and I'd sat still enough hours today already. Pulling over under a street lamp, I reached for the city map I keep in the glove box. Carla Delvecchio's address was not in the Tanoan community but just outside it. I wondered if it would be worth a drive across town. If she wasn't home or didn't answer her door after dark, I'd have wasted the time. On the other hand calling in advance probably wouldn't net me anything either.

Traffic was light; we were on the opposite side of town in about twenty minutes. Carla Delvecchio's home was impressive. Not quite up to Tanoan specs but otherwise a good-sized piece of southwestern architecture. Soft perimeter lighting cast a friendly glow into otherwise dark corners. The reason, surely, was security but the effect was soothing not harsh. Two large arches formed the most dramatic feature of the house, each with an ornate wrought iron light fixture draped into its center. Soft golden light emanated through the colored glass. A single muted chime sounded when I pressed the doorbell.

I could hear faint shuffling sounds as someone approached the door, no doubt checking me out through the peephole before opening it. Carla Delvecchio wore a loose caftan of some velvety looking material in a large pattern of ruby, emerald and sapphire. Her dark chin-length hair looked unsettled, like she'd probably worn it up all day and brushed it loose when she got home. It formed a cloudlike frame for her heart shaped face. The effect was attractive. She was in her early forties with the air of someone who has achieved her desired place in life and is now enjoying it.

"May I help you?" The voice was firm, full of authority and not so concerned with helping me as with getting rid of me. Politely, of course.

"Hi, my name's Charlie Parker." I produced a business card. "I've been asked to look into the death of Gary Detweiller."

"RJP Investigations," she read. "I believe my law firm has used your services. Come in, please."

Now that she mentioned it, I recognized the name. Sloan and Delvecchio. I couldn't remember what services we'd performed. I was sure it had been over a year ago. I stepped into a marble foyer. Her taste in furnishings ran to the classic, with quality wood pieces and rich upholstered fabrics.

"I was just having a glass of wine," she said, "would you like one?"

"No thanks." One margarita was plenty for one

evening. "But you go ahead." I followed her into a spotless kitchen of pale peach.

She finished uncorking a bottle that sat on the counter, and poured a single glass. Her movements were confident. She wiped the side of the bottle with a sponge and recorked it. Next she wiped at an imaginary spot on the counter, then replaced the sponge near the sink and returned the bottle to the refrigerator. "Let's take this somewhere a little more comfortable," she suggested. "I spent most of my day on a hard wooden chair in court."

She led the way to the living room, where a fire sprang to life the second she turned the gas key. Instant coziness. We sat at opposite ends of a peach colored satin couch and stared at the flames.

"Now, you said this was about Gary Detweiller?" she prompted.

"Yes, I understand he had begun hanging around the country club and had hit on some of the female members."

"Including me." She met my eyes with a firm gaze as she said it.

"Well, yes."

"Otherwise, why would you be here, right?"

"Well, yes." I found her forthrightness a little disconcerting.

"Gary seemed determined to make me one of his conquests the minute he saw me," she said. "It was at one of those Friday night dinner dances. I rarely go to them, but that night I had an out of town client to entertain and the club seemed more his style than bar hopping." She paused to sip her wine. "Anyway, I saw this sleazy-looking guy in a cheap suit across the room. My first thought was to wonder what he was doing there. I guess he caught me staring and misinterpreted. The next thing I knew he sidled across the room — pardon me, but that's the only word I can think of for that walk of his."

"I gathered you two got kind of friendly."

"I'd had a few drinks, and I guess I figured what the hell. I laughed at his jokes, but I don't think he figured out I was really laughing at *him*. You know, the whole picture, the moves he made, the image he gave off. He was just so phony." She chuckled slightly as she remembered. "He was obviously there to hit on the rich women. I mean, it was so obvious it was comical."

"Some of them fell for it, though, didn't they?"

"I guess so. Like I said, I don't hang around the club much. It's an image place. Unless there's a business benefit in it for me, I'm really not into projecting an image. I put a lot of myself into my practice, and what little time is left I like to spend alone, recharging my batteries." She took a deep breath and watched the fire dance.

"Anyway, about Gary," she finally said, bringing herself back to the question.

"Who else did he hit on?" I prompted.

"Brad North's wife, I think. She and Gary looked pretty cozy one night. You know him? North? He's a personal injury attorney. I know I shouldn't say this about a colleague . . ." Her mouth formed a little grimace. "But that man is just so obviously after a buck. Get him in a social situation and he's still selling. He'll practically ask you if you've been hurt somewhere, just so he can suggest suing someone. I've never really gotten to know her, but it wouldn't surprise me if she had to look elsewhere for a little attention."

"I was engaged once to Brad North," I told her.

"Oh, God, I'm sorry. I mean for what I said. That was really tactless."

"No offense. I'm thankful it didn't work out. He and Stacy eloped right under my nose. I guess that should have told me what kind of person he is."

"You're right. If you don't mind my saying so, you got the better end of the deal."

"If you don't mind my saying so, I agree." We laughed, breaking the uneasy moment.

"So, who might have killed Gary Detweiller?" I asked.

She sipped more wine and stared into the fire, thinking. "You're investigating on behalf of Stacy North, aren't you?" she asked.

I nodded.

"Well, I don't think she would do it. I don't even know the lady, but it doesn't seem like it would be her style."

"Can I tell you something in confidence?" I asked. "Detweiller stole a watch from Stacy. When she realized it, she was terrified. She had me recover the watch, and I thought that would be the end of it. When he turned up dead, she was even more terrified. I don't think she did it either. But she's scared to death of her husband."

"And she might kill to keep him from finding out what was going on?"

"No! I mean, I really don't think so."

"You don't want to think so."

"I want to find out what really happened, and I want to hope like hell that when I find out, the truth will clear Stacy."

"Could Stacy use a friend in the legal profession?" Carla asked. "I know Brad North, for all his obnoxiousness, has a lot of friends in the business. If she needs a lawyer, she may have a hard time finding one that won't run straight to him."

"She's worried about that," I admitted.

Carla set her wine glass on a coaster and stood up. She stepped into the foyer where I found her reaching into a pocket of her briefcase.

"Here," she said, handing me a card, "have her call me if she needs to."

I took the card and thanked Carla for her time. She promised to call me if she remembered anything more about Detweiller that might point to the killer.

Outside, the air had turned cold. My denim jacket was no match for it. I hurried to the car and turned the heat on. Cold air blasted me until I'd driven a couple of miles. Gradually I began to warm up. It had been a long day and home seemed like a good idea.

Another suspect defused. Another acquaintance of Detweiller who'd claimed to see right through him; who hadn't been taken in or threatened by him. So far, I had to admit, it looked like Stacy was the only one with a strong motive for wanting him out of her life. Someone was lying to me. Who? And why?

11

Who was lying, and why? Who and why? My sleep was filled with faces. Unfamiliar people who taunted me with untrue stories. Hatred and greed and threats and unfulfilled promises loomed as motives. I awoke at dawn, exhausted.

Rusty raised his head as I swung my legs over the edge of the bed. I rubbed at my temples hoping to dispel the headache forming there. He relaxed again on his rug at the foot of my bed as I stumbled toward the bathroom. I turned on the hot water full blast and let it begin to steam as I stripped off my underwear. Adjusting the water temperature downward somewhat, I stepped in and let the stinging spray wake me up. I slicked shampoo over my hair, scrubbing my scalp until it was tender.

Twenty minutes later I was pink and smarting but no closer to any answers. I slipped on a thick terry robe and padded to the kitchen to start some coffee. Rusty dashed out the back door, and I raised the window shades on the back door and above the sink. By the time I dried my thick hair and put on jeans and a sweater, the coffee and Rusty were both ready. He came in and munched down a bowl of nuggets while I stood at the refrigerator door trying to decide what I was in the mood for. I was in the mood to dump this case and take a vacation.

The morning paper waited on the porch. I flipped through it page by page while I worked my way through two cups of coffee. Wistfully, I eyed the ads for spring break trips to Mexico or Hawaii. Once this case was over, I was going to think seriously about traveling. Ron had taken a ski vacation at Christmas and had only gotten out of his cast three weeks ago. His being out of the office had put an extra burden on me for two months. His business trip last week had landed me in the middle of Stacy's problems. I owed it to myself.

That decided, I felt hungry enough to eat a piece of cinnamon toast. I flipped on the radio while the butter and sugar bubbled fragrantly under the red element in the toaster oven. I dumped the coffee grounds and rinsed the pot. Just as I turned off the water, I caught the announcer's words saying that a suspect had been picked up in the Detweiler murder. A prominent attorney's wife.

The shit was about to hit the fan.

I dialed Carla Delvecchio's office and got an answering machine. It was only seven o'clock. I decided to go to the office and try again later. I'd no sooner wrapped my toast in a napkin than my phone rang.

"Charlie?" Stacy's voice was thin and frightened.

"Stacy, where are you?"

"In jail," she cried. "I'm so scared, Charlie. Please help me."

"Does Brad know?"

"Not yet. He had a breakfast meeting at six. The police showed up about five minutes after he left."

"Shall I try to find him?"

"No!" Her voice was terrified. "Can you just get me out of here?"

"Stace, you need an attorney. Let me get you one, and we'll see what we can do."

"Please don't tell Brad," she begged.

"He's going to find out, Stace. There isn't any way to hide this now. But I'll get you another attorney and we'll see what happens next."

She was crying openly when I hung up. I looked up Carla Delvecchio's home number. She sounded barely awake, but agreed to meet me at the police substation where Stacy told me she'd been taken. Rusty didn't look too happy when I told him he'd have to stay home, but I had no idea where this day would take me.

I called our office and left a quick message on the answering machine for Sally and Ron.

The Osuna substation of the Albuquerque Police Department is only a couple of miles from Stacy's house. For me, though, it was over forty-five minutes in morning rush hour traffic. I dashed through the door of the one-story brick building, frazzled and impatient.

"Stacy North was brought in here this morning," I explained to the officer at the desk. "She called me for help."

The officer was an Hispanic woman about my age, who looked like she'd just come on duty and hadn't had her first coffee yet. She pawed through some folders on the desk before thinking to check the computer.

"Oh, yeah," she said, like the name had finally registered with her. "You must have just missed them."

"What?"

"Her attorney came, but they have to take her downtown first. She'll be held there until her bond hearing."

Great. Well, Stacy was in Carla's hands now. I didn't see that there was much else I could do at this point. At a pay phone attached to the wall of the substation, I placed another call to Carla's office. I left a message on the machine to have her call me at my office when she was through downtown. It seemed there was nothing left for me to do but wait.

I climbed in my Jeep and began the slow trek back across town. Today, the air held the promise of spring. Clear blue sky, uninterrupted by clouds, allowed the sun to warm the air. Tree branches were still bare, but thick buds had formed on them, a hint that flowers would soon burst forth. I traveled Osuna Road from the substation west. The golf course on my right showed a hint of green. In the planter areas of the median, the daffodil sprouts were already four inches tall. I wondered where Stacy was right now.

At San Mateo the traffic was thick. Drivers yawned behind the wheel as they inched their way forward. I waited my turn at the light, cutting across three lanes once I got a break so I'd be in the correct lane to turn left at the freeway entrance two blocks ahead. On I-25, things weren't moving much faster. It was impossible to tell whether construction work or an accident was the cause or if this was simply the norm on a workday morning. I stayed in the middle lane, hoping to be in the right place should there be a blockage ahead. Impatient drivers darted in and out, gaining the advantage of a car length or two, only to wait again as their chosen lane slowed to a stop. One blue import passed me three times this way, its driver looking like a prime ulcer candidate.

Somewhere around the Candelaria exit, the flow picked up. The reason was unclear — we'd passed no accidents or other obstructions. I switched to the right lane, ready to join the mini-group that would head west on I-40. I took the 12th Street exit and arrived at the office about ten minutes later. It was still early. Ron's car was in its usual spot; Sally hadn't arrived yet. I caught up with Ron in the kitchen, where he was fumbling to extract a coffee filter from a tightly pressed white stack.

"I hate these things," he grumbled. "Why don't they make them easy to get apart?"

"Want some help?" I took the stack from him, licking my thumb and index finger. Even at that, it took a little coaxing to pry the top filter away.

Ron filled the glass decanter with water from the sink while I measured out the ground coffee.

"Stacy North was arrested this morning," I told him.

"I wondered about that," he replied. "I heard something on the radio about 'a prominent attorney's wife'."

"Well, that probably means Brad has the word by now," I said glumly. "Poor Stace. She sounded panicky when she called me this morning."

Ron poured the water into the receptacle on top of the coffee maker and switched the machine on. We stood there without speaking until it began to gurgle somewhere deep inside.

"What will happen to her now?" I asked.

"She's probably being booked right now," he

said. "Then there will be a preliminary hearing. She might get a judge to agree to bail, seeing that she's not exactly a threat to society. Does she have an attorney?"

I told him about calling Carla Delvecchio.

"She's supposed to be pretty good," he said. "Strong on women's causes."

"I just wish I knew what was happening. I hope she'll call me later to fill me in."

Ron slipped his arm around my shoulders. "You did what you could, Charlie." He saw I was in a slump. "Hey, while the coffee brews let me go get cinnamon rolls."

I nodded but had a hard time getting enthusiastic. He was trying, though. I found two mugs in the cabinet while he went out the back door toward his car. Sally's car pulled in just as Ron was leaving so I reached for another mug.

"Hey, how's it going?" Her cheery greeting fell into such a void that she purposely stepped around me to check my mood. "What's the matter?" she asked.

I filled her in on the morning's developments. I'm not usually a moody person, and it worries those around me when I get into a funk like this. Sally was sympathetic, but optimistic. "Look at it this way," she said. "No one like Stacy North is going to spend any hard time in jail. And Delvecchio's good. She'll have your friend out in no time."

I couldn't help but believe her. Looking into

Sally's honest open face with the wide blue eyes, one couldn't do otherwise. We poured ourselves mugs of coffee and awaited the cinnamon rolls. Ron would probably go to his favorite bakery, which was just up Central Avenue in the University area. I told Sally about my idea of taking a vacation while we waited.

"Charlie, that's a great idea!" she said. "Just get away from here, go find a beach somewhere, lie around, meet some handsome guy..."

"Well, that's not exactly in the plan," I told her. "I just want some time out of town. I need to clear Stacy, Brad, the office, and the tax returns out of my head."

"Do it. Call your travel agent this morning."

I hesitated.

"Don't worry. If a call comes in on the Stacy situation, I'll buzz you."

Ron came back just then, and we each helped ourselves to a thick roll, coated with white frosting and sprinkled with finely chopped pecans. I took Sally's advice and settled in at my desk, travel agent's number in hand. Thirty minutes later I was booked for ten days on Kauai. I would leave May first, giving me plenty of time for tax season to be over and plenty of time, I hoped, to get Stacy's problems out of my hair.

"Line two, Charlie," Sally's voice came through the intercom.

"Charlie, what is *with* this Brad North?" Carla

didn't bother with an introduction, but I guessed who it was immediately.

"In what context, Carla?"

"Wow, I just got my butt chewed royally."

"He what?"

"Yeah. He tracked me down by phone at police headquarters. While I was filling out the paperwork to get Stacy released, he proceeded to inform me that he would represent his wife and that I could just take my little ass home."

"What did you say?"

"I told him the choice of representation would be up to my client. That she had already retained me."

"And?"

"Well, he just about blew a gasket over that. We'll see. You gonna be at your office awhile?"

I glanced at my watch. It was close to eleven. "I don't have any other plans," I told her.

"I should have Stacy out of here soon," she said. "I managed a quick hearing and the judge agreed she's not a threat. Let her out on her own recognizance." Papers shuffled in the background. "Anyway, I thought we might stop by your office when we leave here."

We hung up a minute later.

Ron had left on some mission and I checked with Sally to see whether he'd be back soon. I would have liked to have him there when Carla and Stacy came by.

"Don't think so," Sally said. "He said he had a

lunch date."

I wondered if that was date, as in female. It had been a long time for Ron.

Stacy was a wreck when they arrived a little before twelve. Her jogging suit was rumpled, with a dirty smudge across one hip. Her blond hair hung limp and stringy, looking like she hadn't even brushed it this morning. When she saw me a red rim appeared around her mouth and her eyes became watery. Despite everything, we reached instinctively for each other. The embrace only brought out the tears in both of us.

"I must look horrible," she sobbed, wiping at the tears with a dirty hand. A black smudge made a path across her cheek.

"Yeah, you do." I smiled through a wet haze. "Want to wash up a little?" I pointed her toward the bathroom.

"Will she be all right if she goes home?" I asked Carla, once the bathroom door was tightly closed.

We were in my office now, Carla taking the sofa, I behind my desk. Carla shook her dark head, indicating she didn't know. She wore a pin-striped suit, cream colored silk blouse and dark pumps. Her chin-length hair was breezy yet businesslike, a confident and professional lady. If I ever needed an attorney, I'd want her in my corner.

"I really don't know, Charlie. I was completely taken aback by Brad North's behavior on the phone earlier. Even now, I'm not sure whether he meant to convey concern or anger."

I pondered that. It had been so many years since I'd spent any time around Brad, I just didn't know how to read him.

"What do you think about Stacy's case at this point?" I asked.

"At this point," she responded, "I can't say. I haven't seen any of the evidence yet. I need to talk to her some more. See if she'll open up to me."

"I hope so. The impression I get of Stacy these days is that she's built big thick walls around herself. She's not the same girl I used to know."

"One of the associates in our office has a degree in psychology. She's pretty good at getting people to open up to her. Maybe I can find out more than we see on the surface here."

"If Stacy doesn't dump you and take on her husband as counsel."

Carla nodded knowingly. "That's a big *if*."

Stacy emerged from the bathroom looking a million percent better. She must carry a full toolkit in her purse. She had washed her face and hands, applied full makeup, brushed her hair, and had somehow diminished the dirty smudge on her pants. She even smelled of freshly applied Giorgio.

"Wow, I'm impressed," I told her. I can't seem to make that much difference in myself when I'm dressing up for a date.

Carla patted the sofa next to her, indicating that she'd like Stacy to sit. The two clasped hands for a second. I was glad to see they'd hit it off.

"I'd like to review the case with Charlie present, if you don't mind," Carla told Stacy. "Since she's been investigating, I think she might have some valuable input for us."

Stacy nodded.

I spent a few minutes filling them in on what I knew. I pointed out that the police could probably easily provide motive, via the pawn shop's sales receipt on the Rolex, and opportunity because of the time gap between the time of death and Stacy's established time at the airport that night. Means was the missing link. As far as I knew, they had not located the murder weapon. I asked whether either of them knew about this.

"They didn't mention it to me during the questioning," Stacy said.

"It seems likely they would have," Carla added, "if they had the gun. Although they wouldn't be required to confront you with it at this point. I'll find out about that later when they have to disclose their evidence to us."

"Speaking of which," I broke in, "I'm not sure how to bring this up, but is there an *us*? I mean, Stacy, this is up to you but have you officially retained Carla? Or is there a chance you might turn to Brad?"

Stacy turned her eyes first to Carla, then back to me. She looked confused.

Carla spoke first. "Stacy, whether you choose

me or not, I'd highly recommend that you seek outside counsel. Having family members represent each other gets very sticky."

"And," I reminded her, "you'd have to tell Brad *everything*. I remember the way you looked the first day you came in here, and I don't think you want to do that. With someone else representing you, all that can be kept in confidence unless absolutely necessary."

That seemed to convince her. She reached into her purse and took out her checkbook. Apparently, this time there would be no hiding from Brad that she was spending the money. She quickly wrote out a check and passed it to Carla without another word.

"There's another difficult question I need to ask." I posed the question to Stacy. "Are you all right going home? I mean, would you feel safer somewhere else?"

She looked puzzled. I looked at Carla.

"I didn't tell you about my conversation with your husband this morning," she told Stacy.

She related the story, leaving out a few of the choicer words. Stacy seemed to fill in the blanks herself. She leaned against the arm of the sofa, propping her elbow there and gently resting her chin on her hand. She stared out the window for a full minute. A dozen emotions flickered across her fine features.

"No," she said finally, "I'll be okay. Brad won't hurt me."

I wished I believed it but truthfully, I felt that
Brad had already hurt her. Somewhere down inside,
Stacy was hiding a whole lot of hurts.

"How about lunch, you two?" I suggested, trying
to lighten the mood a little. "I can put it on my
expenses." I winked at Stacy.

"It sounds fun, but I've already left two clients
hanging this morning. I better get back to my office.
You two go. Charlie can take you home later," she
told Stacy.

I'd forgotten that Stacy had been escorted from
home in a police cruiser this morning. That had
probably given the Tanoan gossip mill plenty of fuel.
My stomach clenched a little at the thought that we
might encounter Brad there, but I smiled encour-
agement at Stacy. She'd chosen to face him on her
own. Maybe I could stay low-key.

12

We lunched at McDougal's Pub, a boisterous place where I thought Stacy might feel free to talk because there was no chance of our conversation being overheard by others, and little chance we'd run into anyone we knew. The place was meant to replicate an old-time Irish Pub, with hardwood floors, a long wooden bar with brass rail, and framed prints of the Irish countryside hanging on the dark paneled walls. Visually, it came off cute. Audibly, it was something else. With no sound absorbing surfaces in the entire place, the voices and laughter bounced off the walls and echoed through one's eardrums. The effect was like being locked inside a pre-school at recess time, only the voices were several octaves lower.

Stacy was quiet through the meal, picking at her Reuben sandwich, occasionally swirling a french fry through a puddle of catsup but not eating it. Her mouth stayed set in a straight line but her eyes looked weary.

"Stace," I finally broke in, "do you want to talk about it?"

She shook her head, not meeting my eyes.

"What is it? Are you worried about the case, or is it about going home?"

She busied herself with a large bite of her sandwich, shaking her head as if to say neither. It was obviously my cue to butt out. I changed the subject and we finished the meal reminiscing about high school.

The Tanoan community was as dead looking as ever when we pulled through the gates an hour later. The tan stucco giants shouldered side-by-side, their curtained eyes pointed straight ahead, as if to ignore each other's presence despite the fact that they were almost touching. We drove three blocks before seeing another living being. A yard service truck was parked in front of one of the tan mammoths. Three men bustled about like servants, manicuring and trimming. They would be gone in fifteen minutes, leaving the giant trimmed and pretty, if unloved. I pictured my mother planting and tending her rose bushes with love. I supposed that just wasn't done here.

Brad's Mercedes sat in the circular drive. Stacy tensed visibly as we pulled up. I stopped short, in front of a neighbor's house.

"Are you sure you want to do this?" I asked. "You're welcome to come home with me if you need a few days to get yourself together."

She sucked in a deep breath and let it out again slowly. Her eyes remained riveted to the front of the house. I followed her gaze. A front curtain stirred.

"No," she said, "I'll be fine." She darted a quick, tense smile my way. "I better get in now."

I edged the Jeep slowly forward, stopping in front of Stacy's house. I squeezed her hand.

"Do you want me to go in with you?"

"No, no, don't be silly." She forced her voice to be breezy. "Really, Charlie, I'll be fine."

Secretly, I was glad she'd turned down the offer. I watched her walk away from me, squaring her shoulders as she approached the front door. A person's home should be her refuge, her safe haven from the pressures of the world. Somehow, I knew this wasn't the case with Stacy.

Thoughtfully, I drove slowly through the lifeless streets. What did it matter if a person had shitpots of money, I thought, if there was no joy in their lives? What joy could there be in working oneself to death in a high pressure career, just to come home to a house that looked like it had been cloned from that of a neighbor you didn't even know? My heart went out to Stacy but I didn't know how I could tell her so. After all, she'd made her choice.

It was a little after two by the time I reached the intersection of Academy and Wyoming. I remembered that I'd promised Josh Detweiller to meet him after school one day. My timing might be just about right if I headed across town right now.

At the next red light, I pulled my phone book from the back seat. Video Madness, Josh had called their hangout. It was listed on Coal, I guessed about two or three blocks from the school. I hit San Mateo southbound. The weather was beautiful and it seemed to put people in an aggressive mood. I got the one-finger wave from a guy after he abruptly changed lanes in front of me. After nearly taking off my front bumper, he sped ahead and I watched him pull the same maneuver on someone else.

Video Madness was just that, I discovered, when I finally found the place twenty minutes later. The small parking area overflowed with cars of the same vintage as Josh's primer-coated muscle car. A few newer ones dotted the area but not many. For the most part, these kids were from families like Josh's, hard working, many with single parents. Most of the parents didn't drive new cars, much less their teens. Opposite of the neighborhood I'd just come from.

I could hear the dinging, whizzing, boinging of electronic video games even before I opened the door. The windows had been painted over with black paint. I stepped in, my eyes adjusting slowly to the dimness. The jangling cacophony would drive me crazy in about fifteen minutes. A middle-aged man manned the counter, dispensing quarters, soft drinks, and slices of pizza, which were kept warm under two red light bulbs in a glass case. Clumps of teens gathered around two small booths, formica tables with formica benches running along each side. Apparently food was the first priority after school, although the games were getting a fair amount of attention, too.

I spotted Josh alone at one of the games. His eyes darted around the screen following some dreaded aliens. Both hands were busy at the controls, shooting the monsters with deadly precision. His concentration was total. There might not have been another person within miles as far as Josh was concerned.

I circled, trying to stay out of his line of sight, allowing him to finish his game without distraction. It probably didn't matter — a bomb explosion probably wouldn't have distracted him. I parked myself behind and to his left, watching the game, waiting for a break when I might speak to him. It took about fifteen minutes before one of the aliens got him.

"You're pretty good at this," I commented.

His head snapped toward me. "Oh! I didn't even see you there."

"You were pretty intent all right. You must play a lot."

"Yeah, I guess so. Every day." When he smiled, his face became angelic. "Wanna play a game?"

"Well, I've never really tried these much," I admitted. My eye-hand coordination skills are pretty much limited to the computer keyboard and sometimes even that is iffy.

"Come on," he coaxed. He was already dropping quarters into the slot. "Okay, get over here. You've got the red controls."

My mouth opened to protest but he had scooped me toward him by my shoulder.

"Now, I'm player number one, so you just watch what I do." His eyes were again intent on the screen. I tried to watch his hand moves but, truthfully, I hadn't much idea of what he was doing. His turn took about five minutes, then he was finally shot down.

"Okay, you go."

I felt like a spotlight had just been turned toward me. Surely everyone in the room was about to witness me making a fool of myself. I braced my feet the way Josh had done. Suddenly, red bursting lights were screaming toward my man. I grabbed the controls. I fired. I dodged. I got shot down within a minute.

"That's okay. You're just racking up points right now. You'll get two more turns."

Goody.

Josh was back at it — firing, dodging, ducking. His body emulated the moves his video icon made. Maybe that was the secret — really putting your whole self into it. When I finally got a turn again, five minutes later, I tried the same thing. This time my turn lasted a good two minutes. We each had another turn before the game quit. Josh's score was more than triple mine but he was gracious about it.

"C'mon," I said, "loser buys the Cokes."

The tables had cleared out now. Stomachs filled, the other kids had turned to the games.

"I hold a record for that game," Josh told me proudly as we carried our Cokes to a table. "Really. It lists the high scores, and my initials are right there at the top. You can check if you want to."

"That's great," I told him. "I believe you."

Peeling the paper off my straw, I tried to figure out the best way to broach the real questions.

"I guess you didn't really come here to play video games with me," Josh said.

"Did you hear that they arrested a woman for your father's murder today?"

His straw stopped in mid-air. The color drained from his lips. "No!" He seemed frozen, like an actor in a stop-action scene. Our eyes caught for a minute, until he moved again. "Who was it?" he asked.

"Her name is Stacy North. You might have heard of her husband, Brad North."

"Uh, I don't think so." He jabbed the straw down through the little X in the lid on his cup. He took a long drag on the straw before he looked back up and smiled at me.

"Then it's over, huh? They caught her."

"I don't think she did it, Josh. I know this woman

— she was a friend a long time ago. She did know your father, but very briefly. People don't usually kill someone they hardly know."

"Well, then why'd they arrest her? The police aren't stupid. They know more about it than you do, I bet."

"I'm sure they do, Josh. But they don't know Stacy personally." We were both getting a little hot under the collar, so I steered the conversation another way. Obviously, Josh wanted very badly to believe that the killer had been caught. I let it go.

"Look," I said, "I didn't mean to get you all upset. How's your mom doing?"

He blew out a deep breath, then took a sip of his drink before answering. "*She* is doing great. She's acting . . . I don't know."

He fixed his mouth around his straw again. I waited.

"She's acting all weird, Charlie." He drummed all ten fingers on the table rapidly. "It's kind of like. . . kind of. . like she's *happy*." His voice broke slightly on the last word. He got busy with his drink again, keeping his head tilted downward so I couldn't see his eyes.

I glanced around the room, giving him a minute to compose himself. Noise from the video games clanged from every surface. No way anyone else could hear us. The gurgling sound of an empty straw came from across the table.

"Look, I gotta go," Josh said. He was on his feet

already. He slapped his hand down gently on the table in front of me. "Thanks for the game and the Coke."

He headed for the door. I watched his slim back as he affected his teenage boy walk across the narrow parking area. Seconds later, he was out of sight. I remained where I was, sipping slowly at my drink. Our conversation and Josh's reactions kept playing through my mind. He'd been shocked when I first told him of Stacy's arrest. Why? It was almost like he expected it to be someone he knew. He'd been visibly relieved when he found out who it was.

13

My head was jangling in time with the constant ping-ping-ping of the video games. Fresh air was in order. I stepped out into the bright sunlight, squinting as my eyes adjusted. I'd parked down the block. Now I walked the distance briskly, shaking the noises from my ears and the lethargy from my limbs. It had been a long day but it was only about three o'clock. Perhaps I could find out a little more about Jean Detweiller.

The phone book listed Archie's Diner on Central Avenue, I guessed somewhere around the old Albuquerque High School area. I started west and picked up the next cross street, which took me to Central. Passing the old high school was sad. Both my parents had attended school there but sometime in the early seventies it had fallen on hard times. Now a high chain link fence surrounded the grounds and building. Graffiti scarred the dark brick facade and most of the broken-out windows were boarded up. For years the city had discussed various ways to rekindle life in the place, everything from boutique shops to sleeping quarters for homeless people. But, as yet, nothing had come of any of the political talk. So, she sat there, a sad old lady — dead really, but no one quite had the heart to bury her.

I passed Archie's before I realized it and had to circle the block. Three-fifteen. Jean shouldn't be at work until four, which would give me a chance to ask a few questions without her presence.

The building was probably built in the fifties, when crowds of kids in bobby socks and poodle skirts flocked here after school. The front was mostly glass, huge panes of it, separated by aluminum dividers. The glass rose a story and a half, forming a sharp peak at the top. At the back, the roof dropped away sharply in a dramatic scoop, like some inner-city ski jump. The front of the building sat right at the sidewalk, and access to the rear parking lot was gained through a narrow driveway on the eastern perimeter. I pulled in to find one other car in the lot. Two other vehicles, a sagging twenty-year-old Cadillac and a Volkswagen bug with the front fenders missing, were parked near a greasy back door. The employees.

Inside, the decor was original fifties. A counter ran the length of the place, fronted by chrome and red-vinyl stools. An aisleway just wide enough for a waitress with a loaded food tray separated the stools from a series of booths that lined the windows. An angular chrome jukebox stood in one corner, a yellowed Out-of-Order sign taped to its front. A thin man in a shapeless brown coat sat at one end of the counter, hugging a coffee cup between the palms of his hands. A long tendril of smoke from an ashtray beside him trailed purposefully toward the high ceiling, where it joined a bunch of other smoke, forming its own pollution zone. I took a stool at the opposite end.

"Yes, ma'am, what can I get for you?" The man must be Archie. He was sixty-something, round all over, about my height, five-six or so. He wore a white t-shirt, white pants, and white apron, all of which were spotted with grease and food stains that looked several days old. His head was shiny on top, rimmed by closely trimmed white hair. His jowly face was clean-shaven. I became aware of his thick index finger tapping on the counter, waiting for my answer.

"Oh." I had to think a minute. The Coke I'd just finished with Josh had pretty well killed off my appetite. "I'll just have coffee," I told him.

"How about a piece of pie with that? Homemade this morning. Best in town." When he smiled, he looked much friendlier, like an un-bearded Santa.

"What kind?" I felt myself weakening. Maybe I could call this dinner.

"Cherry, peach, or Dutch apple." He waved toward the glassed-in pie case behind him.

"Dutch apple."

"Excellent choice." He turned and picked up a small plate. I watched him dish up the largest piece of Dutch apple. "Little scoop of vanilla on that?" he asked.

"No, thanks. Just the pie."

He laid a fork beside the hunk of pie and set it down in front of me. While he turned to get my coffee, I asked, "Jean Detweiller works here, doesn't she?"

"Yeah, she'll be here in . . . oh, fifteen, twenty minutes."

"How's she doing these days?"

"You mean after her husband got killed?"

"Yeah. She pretty broken up?"

"Jean's a strong woman," he replied. "You know, she didn't miss a day of work."

"Really." I forked another bite of the pie. It was wonderful. "Look, a friend of mine has been implicated in that case. I'm looking into it on her behalf."

Archie wiped the counter, not saying anything.

"I'm trying to get a feel for what happened. Gary had been out of town, hadn't he?"

"I think so. Jean didn't always tell me stuff like that. The other girl on her shift, Sarah, might know."

"The girls stop for a dinner break sometime during their shifts, don't they?"

"A dinner break and two coffee breaks," he grumbled. "This damn government b.s. They gotta have so many minutes break after so many hours work. Jean's real good about it, though." He made eye contact to be sure I got the point. "There's some'll nit-pick that break shit to the letter of the law. Jean'll work on through if we're busy, and take her break later when things slow down."

"Does she have a regular time?"

"Oh, usually sometime between the dinner bunch and the late bunch."

"When's that?"

"Well, let's see. The dinner bunch comes in, say, between six and eight. Mostly neighborhood folks, you know. Then we gotta little quiet time until the late bunch comes. Those're the ones that go out to some doin's or other over at the convention center or, like, some concert at Popejoy Hall. This time of year, we get the basketball crowd, too. After them Lobos play, that bunch is ready for pie and coffee. And we still make regular ol' fountain stuff like sodas, sundaes, banana splits."

I thought about it. Seemed like the ball games and concerts usually ended around ten. So, it was likely that Jean took her dinner break sometime between eight and ten.

"Do the girls eat their dinner here or do they ever go out?"

"When they got free food here?" He chuckled. "Well, a course, sometimes they do an errand or something."

The man at the far end of the counter was standing up so Archie waddled toward that direction.

I chewed thoughtfully on my pie. Jean might have had motive and opportunity. They lived less than ten minutes away. Could that have been the reason Josh almost freaked when he heard a woman had been arrested, until I told him who it was? Then he almost seemed happy. Maybe he suspected his mother had done it. Jean certainly seemed to benefit the most from Gary's death, and she'd certainly been the happiest since. I wondered if there had been an insurance policy.

I became aware of movement in front of me.

"Charlie?" Jean fixed a look on me like, *What are you doing here?*, but she had the good grace not to voice it.

"Hi, Jean. I heard about the pie here, and decided to try it. So this *is* the place you work."

"Yes. This is the place." She was dying of curiosity, and would probably quiz Archie after I'd left. I hoped I hadn't let my speculations show. "Can I freshen that coffee for you?" she asked.

"Oh, no thanks. I gotta get going." I pulled money from my wallet and left a tip on the counter. Archie was clearing dishes at the other end where the other customer had been. "Great pie, Archie," I called out. "I'll have to come back again."

He raised a hand in a little salute and smiled at me. I left with no further explanation to Jean.

Out in the parking lot, Jean's faded blue Honda was now parked next to Archie's Cadillac. The battered beetle was gone. It must have belonged to some unseen employee lurking in the kitchen. I turned, just as a green pickup truck pulled into the lot. It missed me by no more than two feet. The driver and I were equally startled. She jerked to a stop just as I jumped back a foot or so. I waved her on.

She pulled into an empty slot next to Jean's car and that was when it occurred to me that she wore the same pink and gray uniform as Jean's. I walked toward the truck just as her door opened.

"Sarah?"

"Hey, look, I'm really sorry I almost hit you. I just didn't expect anyone to be walking across the lot this time of day. Sorry. Are you okay?" She had an elfin face, so thin that it almost became lost in the mane of blond hair that hung straight down both sides of it.

"Don't worry, I'm fine." I assured her. "You're Sarah Johnson, aren't you?"

"Yeah?"

I positioned myself so I could watch the back door, in case Jean were to peek out. Luckily, no windows faced the parking area.

"I just wanted to ask you a quick question."

Sarah nodded. She reached up and began twisting her long hair into a thick braid while we talked.

"Do you remember last Wednesday night, a week ago? It was the night Jean's husband was killed."

She looked vague. "Well, I remember the next day because we talked about what had happened."

"Think back. How about the night before?"

"Let's see, Thursday night was a Lobo game. Ricky, that's my boyfriend, stopped by Wednesday night to see if I wanted to go with him. But, I couldn't. I told him I was working Thursday."

"What time did Ricky stop by Wednesday night?"

"Umm, let me think." Her eyes turned upward. "Probably about nine. Things are kinda slow then."

"Was Jean working while you talked to him?"

"No, she was on break. I remember because I kept having to interrupt Ricky to do coffee refills." She had finished the braid and reached into her bag for a hair net. Somehow, in one deft move, she scooped up the braid and got the whole thing into the net.

"Did Jean take her break here or did she leave that night?"

"Oh, usually we just take our breaks here. Sit down in the back and have something to drink. She'll always have a cigarette."

"But that night? For sure, was she here?"

Again, the eyes slanted upward. "No. Now that

you mention it, that night she went out. 'Cause usually if one of us gets a visitor the other will watch the customers and take their break later. That night I called for Jean but she wasn't around, so I stayed on and talked to Ricky at the same time."

"Was she gone long?"

"Well, it would have been her dinner break. She had a full half hour if she wanted it. Even though the food here is free, sometimes you just want something different, you know?"

"So, you didn't get to the Lobo game after all."

"No, Ricky was disappointed, but he said he'd try to get tickets for Saturday night instead." She glanced toward the door, which hadn't budged. "Look, I better get inside."

"Yeah, thanks."

"Oh, and sorry about almost hitting you," she said.

I watched her trot toward the door. I hoped she'd go inside thinking about the narrow miss or about Ricky and the Lobos, and not mention our conversation to Jean. I'd thought about asking her not to say anything, but if they were friends that probably wouldn't have stopped her. I started the Jeep, suddenly anxious to be out of there.

The late afternoon traffic was gathering intensity already. I drove back to the office, staying on Central, which is typically less congested downtown than the arterial streets that lead away. I checked the answering machine and found one message, from Carla Delvecchio. I played it back twice.

"Charlie, I need to talk to you this evening." She gave her home number. Something about her tone of voice told me it was urgent, although she didn't say so. I dialed the number but only got her machine in response. I hate answering machine telephone tag so I decided not to leave a message. I'd call her when I got home.

Rusty leaped with joy, almost knocking me over in his exuberance, when I opened the front door. I fed him and let him out for a romp in the back yard. Elsa Higgins' kitchen light was on so I walked through the cut in the hedge.

A warm meaty smell, interlaced mysteriously with cinnamon, greeted me when she opened the door.

"Come in, come in," she said, bustling me across the threshold and closing the door quickly. "I've had this beef stew simmering all day," she said. "Can you stay?" Her blue eyes were eager.

I felt too guilty to tell her I'd just eaten a big piece of pie so I told her I'd have just a tiny bowl.

"Good. Now you wash up and I'll just add another setting to the table here."

You wash up. How many times had she said those words to me in my lifetime? Thousands, I'm sure. Dutifully, I picked up the bar of soap, knowing she'd scold me if I only rinsed. I watched her shuffle about, gathering a bowl and spoon, putting them on the table for me. Her fluffy white head bent low as she checked the place setting and straightened it.

"How was your visit with Paul and his family?" she asked.

"The usual. Did they stop by here?"

"No, not this time." She sounded a little wistful, but I was sure it was only because she'd forgotten how rowdy his kids are.

"They got in late Friday, and spent all day Saturday with friends. I didn't see them that much myself."

"Now, you don't go apologizing for them," she said. "I never was as close to Paul as you other kids."

I grinned out the window. She'd always see us as kids, I supposed.

Despite the pie an hour ago, I found myself able to put away the entire bowl of stew she had ladled up. I helped her clear the plates, and when she brought out freshly baked cinnamon cookies, I managed to get through a couple of those, too. Tomorrow, I promised myself. Tomorrow, I would start counting my calories and exercising.

I told her about the trip I'd booked to Kauai, realizing belatedly that I could have asked her along. She doesn't get out much and that might have been a thrilling trip for her. But the selfish side of me kept quiet. I really was ready for some time completely by myself.

We washed the dishes and chatted for another hour before I remembered that I needed to return Carla's call before it got too late.

The phone rang four times and I knew I was about to get the answering machine, but she finally picked up. She sounded breathless.

"Did I interrupt anything good?" I asked teasingly.

"Unfortunately, no. I just stepped into the house. Let me put this grocery bag down." There was a pause, while I heard a series of clunks and some shuffling.

"There now," she said. "I'm finally sitting down with my feet up. What a day!"

"Sorry, I wouldn't be calling you at home, but your voice sounded urgent."

She took a deep breath. "Well, not exactly urgent, but I thought I'd bring you up to date on Stacy's situation. You're involved."

"What!"

"Let me backtrack. I talked to the police today. Detective Taylor, I think."

"Kent Taylor. Ron knows him."

"Well, don't be too surprised if he shows up at your office tomorrow. Here's the situation. They've been working on Stacy's connection to Detweiler. They know about the watch. And your name's signed on the sales receipt. When you picked it up."

"Oh, boy. What does that mean?"

"Probably only that they'll want to talk to you. Find out how you got involved, what kind of things Stacy told you."

"Can't I claim privileged client information?"

She chuckled. "Sorry, no. A private investigator has no more privileges than any other citizen. And since you aren't even a licensed investigator, well, you know where that puts you."

I told her, as nearly as I remembered it, everything Stacy had told me. "Will that get her in more trouble if I have to tell all that to the police?"

"I doubt it," she said. "I think they already know most of it. Sounds to me like Stacy was more afraid of her husband than the law anyway."

"What about the murder charge? How are they connecting her with that?"

"Well, they still don't have the weapon. They're glossing over that fact but without it they're going to have a real difficult case. They found a nine millimeter casing under some shrubs near the murder scene. There were two shots fired but only one casing found. Either the killer got sloppy, or didn't even try to retrieve them. They're small. On concrete the wind could blow them around. They'll probably cover the scene again just to be sure the other one isn't lying around in a flower bed someplace."

I thought of Jean's burst of yard-work efficiency. What if she'd been cleaning up after herself?

"They'll probably get a search warrant for Stacy's home next," Carla continued. "They'll be looking for a weapon."

"Stacy mentioned that Brad owns guns."

"Well, if one of them happens to be a nine millimeter and if it's recently been fired, I'm sure they'll be just overjoyed to take it in for more testing."

I was quiet, pondering the implications.

"I guess that's about all," Carla said. "Just wanted to warn you that they've made your connection with the pawn ticket."

She said she was beat so we hung up.

Somehow, I wasn't tired any more. I paced. What would they make of my involvement? If they did find a weapon in Stacy's house, could they try to prove collusion on my part? I'd probably been naive, taking Stacy at face value. She might have counted on our past friendship as a means of providing a backup character reference.

I brushed my teeth, showered and put on a terrycloth robe. Rusty climbed onto the couch beside me, laying his large red head on my knee, his brown eyes watching me with silent support. I stroked his head absentmindedly. The next time I glanced at the clock it was after eleven. I rechecked the doors, turned off the lights and headed for my room. Rusty settled onto his rug at the foot of my bed. Sleep finally came but it was broken up by unsettled patches of wakefulness. I opened my eyes around five, unable to fake it any longer.

14

At the office, I pretended to work on some correspondence but truthfully I wasn't getting anywhere with it. Nagging little suspicions filled my head. I couldn't believe Stacy would deliberately set me up. On the other hand, she was desperate. The missing watch might have only been a middle link in the relationship with Detweiller. Perhaps he'd taken it then tried to blackmail her.

Jean Detweiller's face kept coming into the picture, too. Perhaps I should mention my suspicions to the police. Unfortunately, they were only suspicions. I really didn't have any evidence, only a fellow employee who *thought* Jean took a long break that night and Josh's obvious relief when he heard who was arrested.

The front door chimed at nine o'clock. Sally's voice rose in a friendly greeting, then I heard Kent Taylor's muted response. Heavy footsteps clumped up the stairs. Taylor had that same neatly cared-for look, pressed slacks, clean shirt, neat tie. His overcoat hung open in front. The weather outside was marginally cool enough to need one. I still hadn't decided what I would say to him.

"Hi, Charlie." He didn't hold out his hand, so I didn't either.

"Kent." So far we were off to a great start.

He held up the signed sales ticket from the pawn shop encased in a small baggie.

"I suppose you know what this is about," he said.

"Well, I guess it's *about* Stacy North's Rolex watch, which I retrieved for her."

My tone was a little more huffy than I intended and he picked up on it. He stuck the baggie in his pocket and sat down on my sofa, lounging against the back, one arm draped across the cushions. I lowered myself into my desk chair. When he spoke again, he had become good-cop.

"Did Stacy happen to mention to you how her watch ended up at a pawn shop?" His voice was low, conversational.

I had no idea how to play this. Should I open up and tell the whole story just as it had happened, or should I give yes/no answers only when asked a direct question? I felt myself squirming.

"Not exactly," I told him.

"Charlie, let's not drag this out all day." His voice was still friendly. "You aren't implicated in the Detweiller case personally. Right now, I don't even have reason to believe you're withholding evidence."

He placed subtle emphasis on the words *right now*. I squirmed some more. He waited silently, obviously knowing that I was uncomfortable about this.

"Stacy's my friend. I've known her since fifth grade. I *know* she did not kill that man." My voice came out surprisingly firm. I proceeded to relate most of our conversation as it pertained to the watch emphasizing, truthfully, that Stacy was more afraid of her husband than she was angry with Detweiller. I held back my suspicions about Jean.

Kent made some notes in a small spiral. When he looked back up at me, he was smiling.

"That was a nice piece of detective work you did retrieving that watch," he said.

I have to admit I warmed up a little inside. He clarified a couple of points, then left. I turned back to the work on my desk but found it hard to concentrate. As a last resort, filing is a fairly mindless task, easy to do while preoccupied. I picked up the stack of miscellaneous receipts, bills, and customer folders that had been accumulating for a week. There on top lay the receipt for the new tire I'd bought.

Another unresolved question. I still didn't quite believe it was a random case of vandalism. Someone in the bar that night wanted to slow me down. But who? And why? Maybe another visit to Penguin's was in order.

This time I dressed to fit in — faded jeans, sweater, denim jacket. I made Rusty stay home against his wishes and left plenty of lights on so the house wouldn't look deserted when I got back.

Penguin's was hopping when I arrived. I'd forgotten this was Friday night. The small parking lot was completely full so I parked on the side street about three houses down. The five to seven o'clock happy hour was just ending, and two couples passed me on their way out the door. Inside, a jukebox down near the pool tables twanged country tunes with a vivaciousness that rattled ice cubes in the glasses. There were more women here tonight. Most were dressed as I was, casually but ready to party on a Friday night. All the tables were full and people were two deep at the bar. I pressed my way through the crowd and ordered another Bud Light.

"Draft or bottle?" Pete the bartender asked.

"I don't care."

He handed over a brown bottle, which I carried to a slightly more open space between the end of the bar and the pool tables. On the jukebox Garth Brooks quit and Reba McEntire came on with a soft melody full of pain. At least the room quit vibrating.

The pool table in front of me was getting more active by the minute. The game looked like eight-ball. Both players were good. The guy with his back to me was just about to clear the table, but he'd have to make a tricky bank shot to do it. I found myself staring at the cue ball, holding my breath as he drew back his stick. When the ball went in the pocket, the crowd let out a shout. I breathed again. A dramatic-looking redhead threw her arms around the winner. She wore black leather pants that were in danger of splitting, a sequined gold bra-thing, and a black and gold bolero jacket. He put an arm around her waist and swung her around. When he faced me, I realized it was Larry Burke. We were no more than three feet apart.

"Hi, Larry," I said.

He stared intently, trying to place me. The red-head narrowed her eyes and drew herself up to her full height. In heels she was at least three inches taller than either Larry or me. Larry was decked out, three gold chains around his neck and a pinky ring that would have made Elizabeth Taylor envious. His polystyrene hair was perfect, like he'd just pulled it out of the mold and stuck it on his head. He wore denim jeans so tight they made him stand funny and a western shirt of brilliantly colored diagonals.

"You come here often?" I asked.

"Oh. . . yeah," he said, recognition dawning, "you're the chick asking around about Gary."

I took a slug of the beer, struggling not to grimace.

"Hey, I heard they caught the broad that did it,"

he said.

"A *woman* was arrested, yes. But they don't have much evidence against her. She's out already."

"Hm." He seemed disappointed at the news.

The redhead tightened her death grip on Larry's shoulder. He seemed to take the hint.

"Well, see ya," he said. They walked toward the jukebox.

I turned toward the bar where a spot had opened up. I grabbed it. When I next glanced over at Larry and Wonder Woman he was earnestly explaining something to her. He glanced back at me once or twice, then explained some more with even greater vigor. I smiled back at him, making the task all that much more difficult.

"'Nother beer for ya?" I glanced up to see Pete, the bartender, close by.

"No, thanks, I'm still doing great with this." I would never in a million years finish the whole thing, but I planned to get good mileage out of it.

The crowd seemed to change slightly, coming and going after a drink or two. I watched the new faces as they came in. Larry Burke had finished another game, clearing the table without giving the other guy a chance. He managed to separate himself from his gold plated bodyguard for a minute and was standing in the corner deep in conversation with another man. Their heads were close together, the conversation obviously private. Larry looked up just then, saying something to the other guy and pointing toward me. When the other man faced me, I realized he was the same one who'd sat next to me at the bar the last time I'd been here. Interesting.

I quickly turned my back to them, concentrating on a bowl of popcorn in front of me. I hoped he hadn't got a good clear look at me. My thoughts were spinning. Did this have anything to do with my slashed tire? If Larry Burke perceived me as a threat, what did he have to hide?

Pete came back to check on my drink.

"Who is that guy in the red shirt?" I asked. "The one talking to Larry Burke?"

Pete looked over my shoulder. "I don't see anyone," he said. "Which guy?"

I whipped around to look again. Burke, the redhead, and the other man were gone. I scanned the entire room. No sign of any of them.

"That's weird," I said. "They were standing right there, back by the pay phones."

"Maybe they were ready to leave." Pete shrugged it off. "There's an exit back there. You know, one of those doors that won't open from the outside, but you push on the bar inside and you can get out. Fire exit. Required by city code." He went back to wiping the bar. I sat there wondering what they had been talking about.

I thought back to the last time I'd been here. Pete had mentioned the man's name to me, the one who sat next to me. It had been . . . something easy . . . something like Bill. No, Willie. That was it. And when Willie had got up to leave he'd made a phone call first. Suppose he knew that Larry Burke was somehow involved in Gary's death. If he didn't like my asking questions, might he have called Larry to report this? Since I'd already questioned Larry maybe it worried him. Maybe he'd told Willie to scare me. Maybe by slashing my tire. An uneasy flutter went through my stomach.

I didn't like the way they'd disappeared so quickly just now, right after they'd talked about me. Paranoia rose within me. I thought about my vehicle parked up the street away from the lights and the people coming and going around the bar. I didn't like the idea of walking out there alone, but I didn't want to hang around all evening and give anyone time to cook up something really bad. My eyes darted around the smoky room for answers.

A couple near the door stood up and began putting their coats on. This might be my chance to have an escort out. I hesitated — I'd really wanted to ask Pete a few more questions about Gary Detweiller. The couple were saying goodbye to their table-mates. I grabbed my jacket and pushed through the crowd. They were at the door, and the man graciously held it open for me along with his date.

Outside, the wind bit into my legs ferociously. The storm front predicted for tomorrow was here early. It was one of those March storms that could bring anything — snow, rain — in this case, sand.

The grainy stuff whipped through the air blasting everything in its path. I turned my back to the gusts but not quickly enough. My eyes involuntarily slammed shut, filled with painful granules.

I stepped back into the small alcove by the door, rubbing carefully at the corner of each eye. The other couple had dashed for their car. Its tail lights were already at the driveway. I glanced up the street at my car. Light from a streetlamp across the street illuminated it fairly well. It appeared undisturbed, alone. My fears began to seem unfounded.

A fresh gust slammed into my back, whipping my hair across my face, chilling me through the thin denim jacket. I stepped back into the shadows again, scanning the parking lot. No sign of my three mysterious friends. The hell with it, I decided. If someone wanted to lurk in this weather to get me, they could just lurk a while longer. I stepped back inside.

Penguin's crowded, twangy atmosphere felt warm and friendly this time. I pushed back toward the bar.

"Oh, I didn't know you were coming back," Pete said regretfully. "I tossed your beer."

"That's okay," I assured him. "This time I think I'd just like a glass of water." My teeth felt full of grit.

"Sure thing. Spruce that up with a lemon wedge for you?"

The cold water tasted so much better than the beer that I drank heavily from it and asked for a refill.

"Looks like we've hit on your favorite," Pete grinned.

"I'm not much of a beer drinker," I admitted.

"I knew that the other night," he said. "Was kinda surprised when you ordered it again tonight."

"You're pretty observant." I raised my glass to him. "Tell me more about Gary Detweiller."

"Never saw the man anyplace but here," he said. "A guy can be a whole different person from one place to the other." He dried glasses, stacking them somewhere below the bar out of my sight.

"In here, he was everyone's buddy, I gathered."

"Pretty much. I saw him lose his cool once."

A new voice chimed in. "Hmmph. I sure saw him lose his cool more than once," the man said. He was sitting on the stool next to me hugging a whiskey between his palms. Long legged and slim, wearing Levis, western shirt, and hat, he was about my age. I must have been slipping not to notice him earlier.

"That's right," Pete said, "you knew Gary didn't you, Toby?"

Toby turned to me and touched the brim of his hat. "Sorry, I didn't mean to break in on your conversation, ma'am."

"Oh, please, my name's Charlie." We shook hands. Not even little kids have started to call me ma'am yet.

Toby had an incredibly sexy smile, and I wondered for a flash of a second if he was here alone.

"Tell me more about Gary," I said. "He had a temper, huh?"

"Oh, yeah. Look, I don't mean to speak ill of the dead, you see." The accent was surely west Texas.

I explained how a friend of mine, a real lady, was about to take the rap for Gary's death, and how I needed to find out who really did it.

"If I was you, Charlie, I'd look close to home," he said. "Gary mighta been a real good ol' boy around here, but he didn't extend that courtesy to his family. I was only over there once, now, but I could see he didn't treat that lady of his with any respect."

"That's too bad," I said.

"Why, where I grew up," he continued, "a man didn't never hit his woman. My daddy woulda washed my mouth out if I'd ever talked the way Gary did to that wife and kid of his."

We mused on, discussing the state of the world today with violence gone crazy, both in the family and in the streets. Pete tended his other customers, checking back and adding his opinion every few minutes.

"You know where I think it comes from," Toby said. "I think it comes from a lack of respect. People don't respect anything anymore. They don't respect the law, they don't respect each other or each other's property." He drained the last drop of his whiskey. "I don't know where that attitude comes from, but that's what it is."

He set his glass firmly on the bar. "Well, folks,

it's been fun, but I gotta go."

"Toby, could I ask you one last favor?" I didn't want to seem like a wimp, but I had the feeling this was one man who wouldn't hold it against me. I explained about my earlier uneasiness over Larry Burke and his companions waiting out in the parking lot. "Could you walk me to my car?"

"I'd be more than pleased," he answered in pure Texan.

When we stood up, I realized for the first time how big he really was. He stood at least six-three, and his shoulders were far broader than I'd guessed. A guy this size should be sufficiently intimidating.

Outside, the wind had not abated. Toby had slipped on a sheepskin jacket, and I pulled my denim one closer around me. We walked quickly. My eyes darted around, looking for any sign of trouble, but I saw none.

"Can I ask you one question?" Toby asked as we approached the Jeep.

I nodded.

"How come a pretty little girl like you be named Charlie?"

I had to laugh. I explained to him how I'd been named after two elderly aunts. Charlotte Louise Parker was a rather unwieldy name for a kid, and since I was constantly defending myself against two older brothers, I was sort of a tomboy. I became Charlie and have been ever since.

He smiled bemusedly. "I'm gonna have to tell

that one to my wife," he said. "Her name's Samantha Jo."

"And everyone calls her Sam?"

"Well, no. We all call her Samantha Jo."

I laughed at the puzzled look on his face as I got into my car. I thanked him for the conversation and the bodyguard service, which he shrugged off. Locking my doors, I started the Jeep. As I pulled away, I saw him in my rearview mirror walking back toward the parking lot.

It wasn't until I was nearly home that I realized someone was following me.

15

Lomas Boulevard is a major street, crowded with traffic even at midnight. It hadn't occurred to me that one of those hundreds of other cars might have its sights on me. I drove west, my mind flitting over a variety of subjects not the least of which was how good it would feel to fall into my own comfy bed.

Lomas merges with Central just a few blocks east of my neighborhood. More cars joined us there. I maneuvered across three lanes of traffic into the left lane, ready to turn south at Rio Grande. Maybe because it is a tricky move, one that has to be accomplished in a short space, I became aware that another vehicle had done the same thing. As I waited for the light to change, I glanced back. The strange dark pickup truck edged closer to me, the driver gunning his engine then hitting his brakes so the vehicle pounced at me in little jumps. I edged forward, already across the white crosswalk line. My mind went into high gear.

I didn't dare drive straight home. I tried to think — police station, fire station — where could I go? I thought of the crowds in Old Town. Usually it was packed with tourists but this time of year, this late at night, it would be deserted. I couldn't think of the nearest fire station. The closest police station is downtown, the headquarters. Although there are always people coming and going, it's a difficult place to access. I didn't think I could just pull up to the door and honk. What to do? Think. Think. The light changed.

Without any forethought, I stepped on the gas as hard as I could. The Jeep leaped forward, and I yanked the wheel sharply. Horns blared at me as I cut off the cars to my right who were going straight through the intersection, expecting me to turn left. I kept the gas pedal floored. Once I'd cleared the cars I'd so rudely dashed in front of, I glanced back. My pursuer was in the middle of the intersection, trying to follow my move, but unable to yet because of the three lanes of cars rushing past him. My heart pounded.

Just ahead, the road curved to the left and I lost sight of my foe. I knew, though, that he wouldn't give up. The first break in traffic he'd be after me again. I steered toward the far right lane. I knew we'd cross the river soon, and unless I made a move now, I'd be trapped on the west side, unfamiliar territory to me, with limited means to get back across.

I took the next side street I came to, with no idea where this would take me. I passed some apartment buildings where groups of teens lounged around cars. I didn't take the time to see what kind of merchandise passed between them, but I had a fairly good idea. I didn't want to be lost in this neighborhood. The street came to a T and I debated my choices. Took a right. This one wound in a series of curves, which I guessed were taking me north. My eyes darted constantly to the rearview mirror. No lights appeared yet. My only hope was that my pursuer hadn't seen me turn off Central. If he had, the rest would be easy. I hadn't made an unpredictable move since then.

I continued to wind through the narrow residential street as fast as I dared, praying like crazy that it wasn't a dead end. Eventually, the houses became a little larger, a little more pretentious. Street lights were few and far between here. I had no idea where I was but at least no headlights followed, yet.

Ten or twelve blocks had probably passed. The street continued to meander. Occasionally, I came to cross streets, but had no idea whether they would lead deeper into the maze or which one might eventually take me out. Almost abruptly I came to a major street. Rio Grande. Okay, now I could figure out where I was. The six lanes were deserted. I must have traveled quite a distance. I turned right.

Within a block I recognized a business, a small hardware store, closed now with only a few security lights on. I was less than a mile from the spot where the dark truck had leaped at me. Traffic picked up as I approached Central. I took it cautiously, realizing that my pursuer might have lost me, come back to this spot, waited for me to show up. Which brought another disturbing thought. Did they know where I lived?

I scanned the intersection of Rio Grande and Central as I approached. No sign of a dark truck. Past the intersection, I began watching my rearview. Still nothing. I relaxed only a little. My thumb reached for the control to my garage door opener as I neared the house. The door was open by the time I hit the driveway and I pulled in without a pause, closing the door before I even shut down the engine. I sat there a minute before taking the key from the ignition and reaching for my purse. I was shaking, only partially from the cold.

Rusty greeted me joyfully and I spent an extra few minutes deriving warmth from him. Before doing anything else, I checked the doors and windows. All secure. I kept my jacket on while I made hot chocolate. I gave Rusty a rawhide chew and we took our treats into the living room. The hot chocolate warmed my fingers and my insides finally calmed down.

In retrospect the incident receded in importance. Really, there had been nothing about the truck that I could positively connect with the case. They might have just been trouble makers seeing a lone woman out late. Maybe they only meant to scare me. Maybe they meant to rape, rob, and shoot me. It happens. But the point was, they were probably strangers. I'd gotten away. I counted myself lucky.

I dozed on the couch, waking sometime later to find the lights still on and Rusty asleep beside me. The house was chilly. I had a terrible crick in my neck. I stumbled to the bedroom, switching off lights, peeling off my clothes as I went. I fell into bed naked, not even taking time to brush my teeth.

Something warm and wet stroked my fingers. The sensation blended into my dream, making me feel curiously sensuous. I stretched and rubbed my body against the smooth sheets. The warm stroke came again.

"Rusty!" I woke up enough to realize he was licking my hand, wanting outside. "Go away." I pulled the comforter over my head, tucking in so he couldn't reach me. It didn't work.

He jumped up, front paws on the bed, nudging with his nose at the pile of covers. This signalled eminent danger. If he didn't get outside soon, I'd pay. I forcefully dragged myself from under the covers, and reached for the robe on the back of my

bathroom door. I had barely pulled it on by the time
we reached the back door. Rusty was out in a bound,
and I closed and locked the door behind him.

Sleep came again easily. When I awoke this time
it was almost nine. I felt refreshed and not the least
bit guilty. Stretching luxuriously, I allowed myself
to snuggle deep under the comforter, under no pressure to get up yet. I realized I'd thought of nothing
but the Detweiller case for over a week now and I
was tired of it. Tired of worrying about Stacy and
Brad and Jean and the whole lot of them. I gave
myself permission to take the weekend off.

Bright sun filtered through my bedroom drapes
like a good omen. I peeked outside to spot Rusty
lying on the back porch, patiently awaiting breakfast. The sky looked like smooth blue porcelain, all
traces of last night's storm blown away. Last night's
shadows, too, had receded in my mind. My spirits
perked up with fresh optimism.

Steaming water coursed over me as I indulged
in a long shower, making Rusty wait a few more
minutes. I dressed in jeans and t-shirt, pulled my
hair back into a ponytail, made my bed and tidied
the room. When I reached the kitchen and peeked
out again, Rusty stood with his nose aimed at the
crack in the door, his tail swinging wildly. He wrig-
gled through and planted himself in front of the sack
of dog food.

"Okay, I get the idea," I laughed. I tried to hug
him but, intent on only one thing, he twisted out of

my grasp.

I scooped out nuggets for him, which he set upon like it was the last food on earth. I mixed batter and heated the waffle iron, a special treat for myself. Outside, I noticed there were daffodils already blooming in the back yard. When had those come up? Yes, I vowed, as the toasty waffle scent drifted from the iron, I'm going to enjoy the weekend and not think once about Stacy North.

It was easier said than done. She showed up on my doorstep just after noon.

I'd spent the morning in the back yard. With its eastern exposure, the sun was nice and warm. I raked the winter's dead leaves from the flower beds, pruned the rose bushes back, and watered everything long and deep. The lawn wasn't nearly ready for its first mowing yet, but I'd soon need to contact the teenage boy who usually does it for me. I cut a large bunch of daffodils, enjoying their heady fragrance, then decided I was ready for a lunch break.

The doorbell chimed just as I stepped into the kitchen. I laid the flowers in the sink and pulled a paper towel from the roll to wipe my hands. The thought went through my mind that it would either be someone selling magazines or a Girl Scout. I hoped for the latter — I'm a sucker for those cookies.

Stacy jumped slightly, as though startled from a daydream, when I opened the door. She wore silky-looking pleated slacks in a soft taupe and a cream colored silk blouse with gold buttons. It had some kind of crest embroidered in gold on the breast pocket. Her leather shoes and purse were exactly the color of the slacks. I looked down at my own jeans, which now had round dirt patches on both knees. My t-shirt had taken a dousing from the hose along the lower edge, and was now clinging frigidly to my hip. I didn't want to imagine what my face must look like.

"Hi, Charlie," she said. She turned slightly and glanced over the front yard, taking in the shrubs near the door and the ivy hanging thick around the porch. "Everything's so much bigger than I remembered. The yard, I mean."

"Well, it's had ten extra years to get that way," I replied. It came out a little sharper than intended. "Look, come on in," I invited.

She slipped past me, sleek and graceful as a cat. Stacy had always possessed a certain chic that I lacked. Maybe it was inevitable that we would turn out so differently; it wasn't just her money. In reality, I had money too. My parents, in addition to the house, had left me a decent inheritance. It waited patiently, growing in a trust fund for me until I turned twenty-five. Aside from the money I'd taken out to start RJP the rest was still there. I tend to forget about it. By the time I decide to retire, I'll be able to do it in style. Until then, well, I'm happy with my life as it is. Money obviously hasn't brought Stacy anything I'd want.

"Come on back. I was in the kitchen." She led

the way, pausing to run her fingers over the dining table and to notice the china cabinet.

"You still have a lot of your mother's things, don't you?" she commented. Her voice was almost wistful.

I offered her a cold drink or some lunch.

"No, I can't stay. I'm supposed to be shopping. I'll have to get home soon."

I had picked up the daffodils and was reaching into the cupboard for a vase. Even with my back turned I could hear a weariness in her voice. I glanced at her. The light in the kitchen was brighter, and I noticed for the first time how haggard her face had become. Under the perfectly done makeup, Stacy was close to cracking. I set the vase and flowers down and went to her.

Putting my arms around her felt like hugging a bag of sticks. Her shoulders were so thin. She felt as insubstantial as a bird. Her fingers were icy against my back.

"Come here, sit down." I led her to the table and pulled out a chair. "Now, like it or not, I'm making you a cup of tea." For lack of anything better to suggest, I fell back on Gram's belief that a cup of tea will fix anything.

While we waited for the water to boil I sat across from her. "This has been rough, huh?"

She nodded, tears threatening to overflow. I brought the tissue box and sat again.

"Look, we're going to find out who really did it,"

I assured in the most positive voice I could muster. "It'll all be over soon. I promise."

Stacy dabbed at her eyes, quickly, like she didn't want me to know she was really doing it. Her eyes were dull, resigned. She nodded in response to my promise but she knew finding the real killer would not make it all better.

The kettle whistled and I fetched cups, spoons, sugar, and tea bags. The ritual kept me busy for a few minutes. Stacy remained silent. I laid everything out on the table. Busy-work to postpone what I really wanted to say. I sat again, watching her release a spoonful of sugar into her tea and stir it until I thought she might scrape the bottom out of the cup. I placed my hand over hers.

"Stace. Come on. You can't hold this in forever. Those walls of yours have become thick and impenetrable. Someday you'll have to let someone inside."

The eyes threatened to overflow again. She blinked and wasted some time with her tea, first blowing on the surface of it, then taking a careful little sip. I waited, averting my eyes to give her a tiny measure of privacy. The silence stretched on.

"Stacy, is it Brad?" I finally asked. It was the question that had been on my mind all along. "Is he abusive?"

She set her cup down and straightened in her chair. "Oh, no, Charlie. He's never hit me."

"That's not what I asked. Abuse doesn't always mean hitting."

The tea cup came back up and she got real busy again.

"Okay, you don't have to tell me. Maybe this is awkward for you. But think about it. If he undermines your self esteem, if he belittles you, humiliates you in public — Stace, he has no right to do that. You can get help." I was getting a little out of my depth because I really didn't know what to suggest next, but at least I'd put the thought in her mind. She'd have to decide what to do with it.

We drank our tea in silence for a couple of minutes. Stacy appeared thoughtful but it could have just been her way of blocking out my words. I had no clue from her.

"Hey, I never asked what you came to see me about," I said, finally breaking the silence.

"Oh, I don't know," she replied. "I guess it was nothing really."

She stood up, ending the visit. Near the front door, she stopped to hug me again.

"Thanks, you *have* helped," she said.

I watched her get into her Mercedes and back it out of the driveway. I wasn't sure how I'd helped. Then again, you can only lead a person so far. Any real change has to come from within. I tried to put Stacy out of my mind while I arranged the flowers in a vase, tidied the house, and changed into clean jeans. I wanted to forget about her as I watched a movie on television and while I read a book on Sunday. But her face haunted me for two days.

16

Monday morning dawned with all the prospects of an ordinary new work week. I rose, showered, dressed, fed the dog, and brought in the paper. I poured cereal in a bowl, sliced strawberries on top, added milk and opened the paper.

And that's when I learned of Jean Detweiller's death.

Her picture stared up at me from the front page. An old picture but distinctly Jean nonetheless. I gaped at her thin face with the outdated hairstyle for a full minute before realizing that I could learn more by reading the story.

The phone rang, startling me out of my chair. It was Ron.

"Have you seen the morning paper?" he asked.

"I'm just now looking at it. I haven't had a chance to read the story yet."

"Well, I've had a call from Kent Taylor already. He'd like to talk to our client but it seems she's nowhere to be found."

"What?"

"Just that. She hasn't been home for two nights, and her husband says he doesn't know where she is."

I was having a hard time digesting all this. I told Ron I would read the article and talk to him later at the office.

The paper said Jean had been shot sometime around midnight Sunday night, as she left work at Archie's Diner. Her body was found beside her car in Archie's parking lot. No one had heard anything. The article mentioned the tragic shooting of the victim's husband less than two weeks earlier. The reporter speculated as to whether the two deaths might be connected but no conclusions were given.

My cereal had gone soggy. I picked out the berries and a few palatable flakes and flushed the rest down the disposal. Locking the back door, I called Rusty and gathered my briefcase and jacket. We were out the door five minutes later.

At the office, things were hopping. Ron and Kent Taylor were deep in conversation in Ron's office when I walked in.

"We've got an APB out on your client," Kent said

without preamble.

"Why? What's going on?"

"She's still under arrest in the Gary Detweiller case," he reminded. "And now we want her for questioning in Jean's death."

"Surely, you don't think. . . I mean, Jean might have been a victim of random violence. That's not the best part of town. Violence is everywhere nowadays."

"We have every reason to think," he interrupted, "that there's a connection."

"They've compared the bullets," Ron said. "Both Jean and Gary were killed by a nine millimeter weapon."

"Of course we'll do ballistics tests to be sure if it was the same gun," Taylor added.

I digested this for a minute. "I thought you got a search warrant and checked the North home for weapons last week," I asked Taylor.

"We did. Didn't find the weapon, obviously. But that doesn't mean Stacy North doesn't own it. She could have it in her possession right now. And if she does. . . you can tell her this if she contacts you . . . if she's carrying a weapon, it's a violation of her bail conditions and we'll have her back in the can so fast she won't know what hit her."

It was the longest speech I'd ever heard Kent make. And it wasn't especially reassuring.

"Stacy came to see me Saturday morning," I told him.

"Why didn't you say so?"

"I was just about to." Now that I'd opened my mouth, I wasn't sure how much to tell. Stacy's marital problems weren't part of this, at least not directly.

"Well?" Kent and Ron were both watching me.

"Well, she didn't tell me she was going out to kill Jean Detweiller," I snapped. I made myself take a deep breath. "She was upset, but we didn't talk about the case at all. I gathered her problems were personal. Her husband is a difficult man to live with." Understatement.

"Was she angry, defiant, or what?"

"Not at all. Depressed was more like it. She spoke very little and was on the verge of tears the whole time. If Stacy North left with the idea of killing anyone, it was probably herself."

Even before the words left my mouth, I realized their import. "Oh, God, do you think. . . " I turned to Ron. "Do you think she might do something like that? What if I could have stopped her?" My mind was spinning.

Ron rose from his chair and came around the desk. He put a comforting arm around my shoulders.

"Let's all sit down and think this out," he suggested gently.

He led me across the hall to my own office and guided me to the sofa. "Sit here. I'm going to get you some tea."

Kent Taylor was oddly quiet as he took the side chair next to my desk. Ron came back a minute later with coffee for Taylor and tea for me. He sat beside me on the couch.

"Now, tell us about Saturday morning."

I related the gist of the visit, without going into a lot of detail. Stacy obviously didn't even want to talk to me about her marriage. It seemed invasive to bring two more people into it.

"So, you think she was depressed when she left?" Taylor asked.

"I don't know. I'm no psychologist. She was unhappy. Maybe she just decided to go somewhere and be alone awhile."

"Well, you better hope she hasn't left the city. And you better hope she comes back soon."

"Will she be arrested again?" I asked.

"We'll have to question her." He said this as though it would be obvious to a child.

I didn't bother with a response. The conversation was about finished by then and he left a few minutes later.

My desk was stacked with mail that I had not attended to last week. Somehow, though, I just couldn't put my mind to it now, either. I reread the morning's front page story.

Jean had been killed outside Archie's. As far as I knew, Stacy didn't know anything about Jean Detweiller — her workplace, her schedule. I suppose she could have found out, but it didn't ring true.

Stacy had been much too enveloped in her own problems to focus on tracking and killing Jean.

Poor Josh. I thought of the troubled kid who'd now lost both his parents to violence. I had to talk to him. I picked up my jacket. Ron was on the phone, but I told Sally to tell him I'd be out for awhile.

Taking the scenic route up Central Avenue might not have been the quickest path to the Detweiller house. It did, however, lead me past Archie's Diner. I decided to stop there first.

It was past the breakfast hour and the parking lot was nearly empty. I saw Archie dragging a coil of green garden hose from a storage room at the back of the restaurant. He screwed the hose coupling onto a faucet mounted on the back wall of the building and attached a sprayer to the other end. He tried to walk toward the middle of the parking lot with it, but the knot of hose on the ground yanked back at him. A few choice words slipped out as he tried a whipping motion to get the thing untangled.

"Hi, Archie," I called out.

He squinted toward me, trying to place me.

"Charlie Parker," I reminded, "I was here the other day." I was standing one parking space away now.

"Oh, yeah . . . You the one asking about Jean, weren't you? Well, I sure don't know how to tell ya this . . ."

"I already know." We stood silently for a minute, neither of us knowing quite what we should say.

"Um, I . . ."

He gestured toward the next parking slot, and it dawned on me what he was doing. A large brownish stain formed an irregular circle on the pavement. He aimed the sprayer at it before realizing that he hadn't turned on the water.

"Could you get that faucet for me?"

I trotted to the building, glad that the little errand postponed our conversation, even for a short while. The faucet handle was old and caked with dirt. I struggled with it, taking a little longer than necessary. The spritzing sound of water blasted behind me.

"Police said they were done here, so I guess it's up to me to clean this up," he commented when I walked back to him.

"I was really sorry to hear about Jean," I told him. It sounded trite. I'm terrible at these things.

"Yeah, me too," he said. He kept spraying, forming a red puddle that soon turned pink, then ran clear.

"How's Josh doing?" I asked.

He gave me a puzzled look.

"Her son."

"Oh, the boy. Well, gee, I sure don't know. Hadn't given him much thought." He guided the puddle of water out toward the street. "Funny, you know, she didn't talk a whole lot about the family here at work. Kinda like she came here to get away from them. She'd mention 'em sometimes, but not like some of these mothers do, where you hear about it every time the kid goes to the bathroom."

"She didn't say how Josh was handling his father's death then, I guess."

"Nope. Don't tell nobody I said this," he said, leaning toward me as if there were dozens of people standing around, "but I think Jean was so happy with her own freedom that she didn't take time to think about what her kid was doing."

His eyes met mine with a knowing look. I tried to look surprised at his words, but truthfully, I wasn't.

"I thought I'd stop by and visit Josh," I said. "Just to see how he's taking it."

"Good idea," Archie grinned. "Poor little guy could probably use a friend right now."

I wondered if he knew that Josh was sixteen, practically a man.

"Were you here when it happened?" I asked, taking a different tack.

"Nope. It was right when Jean got off work at midnight. I got me a night manager for that late shift." He chuckled in a humorless way. "I'm gettin' a might old for that late night stuff. I can still get right up with the birds in the mornin' but when the late shift comes on, I usually go home."

"Didn't anybody hear the shot?"

"They say they didn't. Hell, in this neighborhood, it ain't that uncommon."

We did a little more chit-chat while Archie coiled

up the hose. He invited me in for another piece of pie but I told him I'd have to make it another time. I drove away wondering how well he'd really known Jean.

The Detweiller driveway was full of cars. Josh's was nearest the garage door, blocked in by three others. Relatives or friends?

I tapped on the door, but the hum of voices inside was loud enough that no one heard. Finally I tried the knob myself and just went in.

Josh sat on the sofa, a pretty blond girl of about fourteen wrapped around one arm. He didn't seem to be paying a lot of attention to her. A middle-aged couple had pulled two kitchen chairs into the living room and sat facing Josh. After pausing to gape at me for a second, they resumed talking in hushed tones. The man wore a dark suit and tie and had a Bible in his hands. Josh shot me a "rescue me" kind of look, but I wasn't about to get into that. I sidestepped the little group, heading in the direction I assumed the kitchen would be.

It, too, had been commandeered by the church ladies. Two of them, in polyester pantsuits, had laid out a spread on the kitchen table that would feed twenty easily. They had a ham, two plates of fried chicken, potato salad, green beans, and various Jellos in several colors. Not to mention two sheet cakes baked in disposable metal pans. The two women smiled at me but I caught them looking at my empty hands. I ducked out the way I'd come.

No one was especially paying any attention to me, so I slunk across the hall into the master bedroom. The thought had come to me, driving across town this morning, that Jean's death could be tied to Gary's because of something she knew. Gary's business dealings were a little on the dim side, to say the least. What if Jean had found out something about somebody and they knew that she knew . . . I wondered if Gary kept any files or papers at home.

The bedroom drapes were pulled, making the room cool and gloomy. I pushed the door shut, guiding it with both hands, turning the knob so it wouldn't make any noise. Alone, I was like a kid in a toy store. What to touch first?

The room was neat by Jean's housekeeping standards. The bed was made. Maybe she was like me, hating to crawl back into an unmade bed; the sheets and blankets have to be smoothed out or it feels icky. The rest of the bedroom was more in keeping with her neatness criteria for the other rooms.

There was no file cabinet with a drawer labeled "Illegal Stuff" so I had to go into this blind. There were two night stands, a dresser, and a chest of drawers. It was anybody's guess. I picked the night-stands first. The first one held an assortment of feminine articles, including a romance novel, three sheets of pink stationery with frayed edges, an emery board, and a diaphragm. I pawed through the contents clear to the back, and only came away with a dusting of powder from some long ago broken compact. Wiping my fingers on my jeans, I went for the second stand.

This must have been Gary's. Two copies of Playboy and a nail clipper. Below the drawer there was an open space, ostensibly for books or perhaps an object d' art. In this case it was crammed with papers. Quite a few were old racing forms and newspapers, shoved into the space with no apparent method of organization. Others were sheets from yellow pads, spiral notebooks, or whatever was probably handy at the time. I recognized Gary's heavy slanted writing on most of them. I began to flatten them out to see if there was any theme to the whole mess.

Just then, I sensed movement from the other room.

"Now, son, I want you to know that you can call on Mrs. Luthy and me just any time you need to. We're here in the Lord with you, in your time of sorrow." The preacher was making his closing statement. Their voices were just the other side of the wall from me. Apparently they were standing at the front door.

"That's right, son," a female voice joined in. "And we'll look for you in Sunday School this week."

I jammed the handwritten papers into my bag and zipped it shut. The racing forms and newspapers went back into the night stand. Judging by the layer of dust on everything, I doubted that Jean had gone through this stuff but there could be a clue here somewhere. Right now I had to get that door open before anyone figured out where I'd gone. I reached for the knob.

Another voice piped up, no more than a foot from my face. "Yes, Josh, we'll see you Sunday." I held my breath, knowing they could probably hear the sweat trickling down my sides right about now.

"We've set lunch out for you, now. You and your friend be sure to eat something." The voices were receding in the direction of the front door.

I turned the doorknob slowly with my right hand, holding my left hand up to the crack as it gradually opened. Like that would keep them from seeing me. Eye to the opening, I held my breath. I could see no one, so I slid the door open and myself out. In a quick switch of directions, I tried to make it look like I was just coming from the bathroom across the hall. One of the food ladies gave me a funny look but didn't say anything.

The three women had their purse straps over their arms, neat cardigans buttoned up tight. Josh stood at the front door, seeing them out. The blonde had kept her seat on the couch. I hung back, letting them finish trying to save Josh's soul. He closed the front door behind them with a sigh.

"Hey, Charlie," he said.

"Hey, Josh." He came toward me, unsure, and we gave each other a brief hug. I told him I was sorry about all this; he murmured something that sounded good. We were both glad to have that part over with.

"You hungry?" I asked. We went into the kitchen.

"Sort of." He eyed the spread on the kitchen table. "I kinda wish they'd brought some Quarter Pounders." We laughed.

"Well, this is here already. Want me to fix you a plate?" I offered.

"Naw, I'll get something later."

The girl was on her feet now, giving me the evil eye, like I had romantic intentions toward her man. Please. I'm old enough to be his . . . his much older sister.

"I'll at least stick the potato salad in the fridge so it doesn't go bad," I said. "If you don't eat soon, you better put the rest of it away, too."

"Okay." The two of them went back to the other room.

"You doing all right?" I asked when I returned to the living room.

He shrugged. "Okay, I guess."

"At the risk of sounding like everyone else, I'd say you can call me if you need anything. But maybe I shouldn't. Just know that you can." I pulled a card from my jacket pocket and laid it on top of the TV set. He smiled but didn't acknowledge the card.

"So, what will you do now?" I asked.

"Whatta you mean? Same as ever, I guess."

"Look, not to put a real damper on things, but I

doubt if the welfare people, or whoever has a say in these things, are gonna let you just live alone. You're still under age."

"Hey, I can take care of myself just fine," he protested.

"I'm sure you can. But I know how this is. My parents both died when I was sixteen, too."

He looked straight at me. "No shit!"

"No shit. Killed in a plane crash coming home from Denver. It was just a quick weekend trip. I'd stayed over with a girlfriend." Stacy. "I thought I'd just go home and run the place by myself, but I didn't have the say-so in it."

"So, what'd you do?"

"Well, I was real lucky to have a neighbor who's like a grandmother to me. She took me in until I was out of school. Luckily, my folks left the house to me, so I moved back into it when I was in college."

Josh was quiet for a couple of minutes. "Well, I sure as shit can't stay here," he said finally. "Not unless I can come up with a month's rent by the first."

The girl had wound both her arms around one of his and stared up into his face now, like she'd love to kiss it and make it all better. He seemed oblivious to her.

"I've got an aunt," he said glumly. "Here in town. She lives up in the northeast heights. I guess I'd have to go to Eldorado." He mentioned the name of the other high school like it was in Iran or somewhere equally friendly.

"It might not be so bad," I said, trying to make it sound better than it really was. Having to transfer to a new school near the end of one's junior year had to be pretty disheartening. "Or wait, what about seeing if they'd let you stay at Highland? I think they do that now. If you've got your own car, which you do, I'll bet it can be arranged."

He cheered up a little at that and decided maybe he was hungry after all. We went into the kitchen and found clean plates. He stacked on four pieces of fried chicken and close to a pint of the potato salad. We carried our plates back to the living room. They took the couch and I perched on the edge of the vinyl recliner.

"Josh, I want to help find out what happened," I said between bites off a chicken leg.

He shrugged, chewing. "Gangs, probably," he mumbled with his mouth full.

"Are you sure? Don't you think this seems awfully coincidental, both your parents so close together? Think. Did your dad have enemies? What about your mom?"

"Maybe some of those guys my dad hung around with," he suggested.

I glanced over at the girl, who had still not said a word in my presence. Josh had not bothered to introduce us. I had no idea what her name was. Maybe it wasn't such a good idea discussing all this in front of her.

"Well, I'll do some checking on it," I said, getting up to take my plate to the kitchen. I put it in the sink and ran water over the sticky places.

Josh sat on the sofa with his plate on the coffee table in front of him. Still packing away the chicken.

"Look, I've gotta go now," I said. "Stay in touch. Let me know when you're moving."

I retrieved my jacket from the back of the vinyl recliner and my purse from the floor behind it.

"I'll talk to you later, Josh." He waved, still chewing.

17

Back at the office not a lot was happening. Sally bustled about in an effort to clear her desk. Nearly one o'clock already. She handed me two pink message slips and her outgoing mail. The messages were for Ron. Sally's jacket hung over her arm, car keys in hand.

Rusty heard our voices and trotted down the stairs to greet me. I scratched his ears while listening to Sally's last-minute explanations.

Upstairs, Ron sat at his desk with the phone jammed against his ear, pinned in place by his shoulder. I noticed a sheen on his head where there isn't much hair. He jotted notes with his right hand while reaching for his coffee cup with the left. He spends so much time this way that he probably doesn't even realize how many things he's doing at once. I dropped the two pink slips in front of him. He raised his eyebrows at me, the only available means of waving he could manage.

Across the hall, my own desk was beginning to resemble a tornado path. Today's mail lay on top of the burgeoning pile. Sally had probably set it there with reasonable care but the whole thing was so unbalanced that it had slid, coming within a quarter inch of falling to the floor. I tossed my purse and jacket on the sofa and pulled out the trash can. I have to confess that I'm not very tolerant of junk mail and three-fourths of the stack went into the can unopened.

Of the remainder, I sorted it into stacks: bills, correspondence and incoming money. I listened to the sound of Ron's voice across the hall, although I couldn't make out the words, while I applied the incoming checks to their respective accounts and filled out a deposit slip. This felt like routine — Ron on the phone, me working on the books.

I posted the receivables to the computer, then ran a past-due report. The usual. A couple of the law firms we work for are notoriously slow in paying. I'd have to send statements. It only took a few minutes to update the records and print the statements.

By three o'clock I'd paid the bills, stuffed the customer statements into envelopes, and run a preliminary trial balance of the general ledger accounts. I made a copy of this for Ron in case he wanted it. He normally just glances at it and leaves it up to me to be sure it's correct. Rusty planted himself on the rug between me and the door, making sure he wouldn't be left behind again. I worked without paying much attention to him until he perked his ears toward the doorway.

Ron stood there stretching. He rubbed at his neck and shoulder where the phone had rested, probably without even realizing he did it. I handed him the trial balance pages.

"I'll probably work on this tomorrow," I told him, "so if you see any problems with the numbers, speak up soon."

"Okay." He glanced at the pages quickly. "It'll make interesting reading while I'm on surveillance tonight."

"Surveillance, huh? Your very favorite part of the job."

"Yeah. Right."

"What? Another errant husband?"

"Nah, this is insurance fraud. Guy who's suing for auto accident injuries. Claims he's totally incapacitated. Company thinks he's faking it. Get this — they think he may try to go bowling tonight."

I gave him a look.

"Yeah, the guy's crazy about bowling. His league's forming up again and they think he might not be able to resist."

"So you get to hang around the bowling alley, or

what?"

"Yup. Hell, the guy's learned to spot my car in his neighborhood, so he's real careful what he does around home. So, Joey and I are gonna put on our old bowling shirts and hang around. I might get lucky. If the guy shows up I've got this little no-flash camera and I'll try to get pictures of him in the act. That oughta pretty well cinch the case."

"You and Joey, huh." He knows I can't stand his buddy, Joey. He lives in Ron's decidedly tacky apartment complex and somehow latched onto my brother as his best buddy. Two divorced guys, commiserating about the exes and their kids.

"Well, have fun," I said drily. "Oh, before you go, have you heard any more from Kent Taylor on the Detweiller case?"

"As a matter of fact, I did. Ballistics confirmed it. The same gun killed both of them. Now they sure would like to find your friend, Stacy." He turned back toward his own office, waving one hand in my direction. A minute later I heard his voice on the phone again.

Stacy. I'd like to know where she was, too.

I finished a couple of other printouts and backed up my data on disk. Ron left and the office got quiet now with him gone. I felt better about getting my own work under control. The past week had seemed disorganized to me. Tomorrow I could take care of the correspondence stack and get started balancing the month-end books.

Rusty and I made the rounds, locking the front door and checking the windows. I unplugged the coffee maker and rinsed out the filter basket and pot. When I shut off the water, I heard Rusty's low growl. I looked down to see the hair rising on his neck. He was staring at the back door.

Behind the sheer white curtain in the upper glass panel I saw a shadow. The glass coffee decanter was the only weapon handy. I clutched it by the handle.

The shadow moved closer, toward the doorknob. Rusty barked and it jumped back. Then a tentative knocking sounded. I tiptoed toward the door. Pushing the sheer drape aside, I saw who it was.

"Stacy!" I jerked the door open. "Where have you been?"

Rusty relaxed and came toward her, his tail waving slowly back and forth. He sniffed at her pants leg.

"Come in," I said, pulling at her. "You almost got clobbered by a coffeepot," I told her, realizing how ridiculous I probably looked clutching the decanter like a club.

She stumbled slightly over the doorsill.

"Stace?"

Her face didn't look right. Her makeup was faded. The clothing which had been so stylish Saturday morning was limp and wrinkled now. She seemed dazed.

"Stace, tell me what's wrong," I pressed. I led

her to the kitchen table and pulled a chair out for her. She fell into it, her shoulders drooping, her expression blank.

I opened another chair out to face her and took both her hands in mine. "Stace. Listen, you need to tell me what's happened."

She swallowed hard and took a deep breath. "I've been hiding out," she said.

"From the police? Oh, Stace, that's a mistake. You need to tell them what happened."

"The police?" She focused on me, confused by what I'd said. "No, Charlie. From Brad. I had to get away from Brad."

"Wait a second. Maybe we better start over. Tell me what happened with Brad. No, tell me everything that happened since I saw you Saturday morning."

She leaned forward, more alert than she'd been. "Saturday morning. I left your house thinking about what you'd said, about how I'd built walls around myself. I decided to find someplace to stay alone that night, to think about it. I found this little bed and breakfast place. It was really peaceful."

"Did you tell Brad where you were?"

"I called, but remember, he was out of town. So I left a message on the answering machine that I just needed to be by myself for awhile. I didn't want to tell him where I was. He would have found the place."

"Go on."

"I guess he came home Sunday morning. I wasn't there and he didn't believe the part about my wanting to be alone. He's very jealous." Her voice got thick at this point. She took a minute to get under control again.

"When I got home that afternoon, he was in a rage. He ... well he was very angry." She just couldn't let go with the details. "I got so scared. I grabbed my purse again and took off. I went back to the place I'd stayed Saturday night. I spent last night there again. Today, I've been wandering around trying to figure out what to do next."

"You mean you weren't aware that the police are looking for you?"

"Police! Why? Charlie, what's happened? Did Brad . . .?"

"It's nothing to do with Brad, Stacy. Jean Detweiller, Gary's wife, was murdered Sunday night."

"Murdered?" She said it like she was trying to remember the definition of the word.

"They want to ask you some more questions," I explained.

"I didn't even know her. How would I know who killed her?"

"Stace, they think you might have done it."

"Me! That's crazy, that's . . ."

"I know, I know." I had to grasp her arm to keep her seated. "But you have to remember, they still think you might have had something to do with Gary's death."

"Charlie . . ." Her voice trailed off. Her eyes were wide with disbelief.

"They've run ballistics tests, Stace. Both the Detweillers were killed with the same gun."

"Well, I don't know anything about any gun," she protested. "I don't know about any of this. This whole thing is a nightmare, Charlie." Tears flowed like streams now. "My whole life is a nightmare."

I located a box of tissues and handed them to her.

"Stace, this place you stayed the last two nights. Surely the people can testify that you were there. Last night, did you stay there all night? You didn't go anyplace else, did you?"

She was already on her third tissue. She pulled another from the box and blew her nose.

"No, I stayed right there. The people were so nice. We visited a little while after dinner, then they went to bed. I stayed in my room and read a book. It was so peaceful, so quiet."

I wondered whether the people who ran the place would testify that she'd been there all night. If they went to bed early, how would they know she hadn't left around midnight and come back? I didn't say this to Stacy.

She'd calmed down quite a bit now. Tissues lay in damp little wads all over the table.

"What now?" she finally asked.

"Well, I think we better call Kent Taylor and let him know where you are."

A panicked look crossed her face, but I assured her that they'd find her anyway.

"They've already been to your house looking for you, so Brad knows. I think they were even going to put out an APB on you. You'd probably be stopped by a patrol car before you got across town. It's better if we call them first."

"I suppose so," she finally agreed.

"You just tell them what you told me. At least the part about the bed and breakfast. Give them the name of the place and where it is. They'll probably want to talk to the people who run it. You can tell as much or as little about Brad as you want to."

She nodded.

"Look, I can call Taylor if you want me to. You want to wash your face and freshen up a little?" We walked upstairs together. I pointed her toward the bathroom and kept an eye on the door while I made the call.

Kent Taylor actually sounded happy to hear from me, once I'd told him who was at this moment in our bathroom. He said he'd be right over.

He showed up with a uniformed officer and a search warrant for Stacy's car and personal possessions. The other officer searched the car while Taylor questioned Stacy. I listened to her story again and it gelled with the first version. I felt fairly sure she was telling the truth. She left out the part about Brad's jealous rage and about the reason she'd wanted to get away in the first place.

It was eight o'clock before they all finally left my office. Rusty and I stopped at a fast food place where we both indulged in cheeseburgers and fries.

At home, I came across the bunch of papers I'd stolen from Gary Detweiller's nightstand. They were wadded and disorganized, and I just didn't have the stamina right now to go through them. I put them on the desk in my home office, held down with a glass paperweight. I showered and fell into bed almost immediately. I was bone-tired but my sleep was unsettled. I had indigestion all night from the greasy burger. I blamed the food, although the stressful day probably hadn't helped a bit.

18

After falling asleep around four a.m., I didn't rouse again until after nine. Somewhere in the back of my memory, I thought I'd had a productive day planned but now I couldn't seem to focus. I showered and dressed in jeans and sweater. I really should go in to the office; there was correspondence waiting, I remembered. But Stacy's plight seemed to loom large. I couldn't help but wonder what had happened when she went home last night, *if* she went home. I speculated as to whether I should call.

Rusty and I went through our morning breakfast routine then left for the office. We arrived to find Ron pouring coffee into his mug with one hand, gripping his lower back with the other.

"So, how was bowling last night?" I teased.

He shot me a look through pinched eyebrows.

"I thought you were there to surveil not to participate."

"Well, you know. It looks kinda suspicious to sit around a bowling alley all evening and never pick up a ball," he explained.

"And Joey just happened to talk you into throwing a few."

"Yeah, well. . ."

"I'm not gonna ask who won. Obviously, your back didn't."

He ignored that and took his coffee to his own office. I stopped by Sally's desk on my way upstairs. She handed me one pink slip. Sarah Johnson. Sarah Johnson. . . Oh, yes, the one who worked with Jean Detweiler. Now what would she have to tell me?

As it turned out, I had to ponder the question awhile longer. There was no answer at the number she'd given. Assuming she still worked the late shift, maybe I could catch her as she arrived at work this afternoon. This left me without much choice but to go ahead and answer the letters that had stacked up on my desk.

By two o'clock I had that nasty little chore taken care of, Sally had left for the day, and Ron was again glued to his telephone. I slipped a note in front of him, letting him know I was switching on the answering machine and leaving. I'd been wondering how Josh was doing, and since the Detweiler house and Sarah's work were so close together, I might as well make one trip of it.

The boxy little house looked all closed up, with no cars in the driveway when I pulled up to the curb. I knocked on the front door anyway. No response. No big surprise. As I stepped off the porch, I saw a lady in the next yard holding the garden hose sprayer over a flower bed. She raised her hand in a little wave.

"Hi," I said, cutting across the Detweiller drive to approach her.

"Nobody's home there," she said. She leaned a bit closer to me. "The man and his wife were both *murdered*."

She didn't say "died" or even "killed." This one liked to get the sensational tidbits right into the conversation. I looked closely at her for the first time. She was in her late fifties, with short gray hair mostly hidden by a wide-brimmed gardening hat of turquoise fabric with pink dots the size of quarters all over it. Her pink garden gloves were nicely color coordinated, although the green slacks and pullover she wore clashed badly with the hat.

"I was hoping to find Josh at home," I told her. "Maybe he's back in school today."

"Oh, I don't think so," she said. "That blond girl was here earlier. I think her name's Casey. They had that music blasting me practically out of my house all morning. Then, about an hour ago they left together."

This woman must do a lot of yard work. She really was up on her neighbor's movements.

"I heard that Mr. Detweiller was killed right here in the driveway," I said. "You probably heard the shot."

"Well, I'm sure I would have, but Wednesday's Buzz and my bowling night. We never get home until after ten. That night, whooee, I mean to tell you, that was some commotion. Those cop cars and ambulance and all, they didn't leave till around midnight. Well, it was ten after, I'd say."

Pegged to the minute, I'm sure.

"What about the other neighbors? Were any of them home?"

"You some kinda investigator?" She narrowed her eyes briefly, scrutinizing me. Just as quickly, she brushed it off. "Well, anyway, I don't know about them others. You know, the people in this neighborhood, they don't look out for each other the way we always used to. I mean, I could be mugged on my own front porch and nobody'd come check on me for a week. Well, just look what happened here." She gestured toward the Detweiller driveway to prove her point.

I nodded, not wanting to slow her down.

"You know what it is? Stereo. That's right. You know they have stereo sound in TV sets now? Yeah. And people play them darn things so loud, why a bomb could go off in their own living room and they'd never hear it." She swung the hose sprayer toward

an evergreen at the other side of her own driveway
and I had to trot around to keep facing her. "Nope,"
she said, "I'm not a bit surprised no one heard that
man get killed."

We edged our way through her front yard, each
shrub getting a minute or two under the shower.

"Now me, if I'da been home, you can bet help
woulda come that much faster. I'da heard that shot."
She leveled a knowing look at me. I believed her.

"Well, I guess I'll try to catch Josh later," I said,
somewhere between the lilacs and the roses.

"That poor boy." She pulled her upper lip down
between her teeth, sharing his pain vicariously.

"I'm sure he'll have a tough time of it," I said.

"He's already had a tough time of it. They was
always chewing on him for something."

"He'll probably go live with his aunt, I hear."

"I don't know if I've ever met the aunt," she said.
"Well, she can't treat him a whole lot worse than the
parents. And they kept such weird hours. You know,
that mother was out all night. Every night." She
tsked over this, like working a night job should have
been on the list of mortal sins.

We'd just about made the rounds of the whole
front yard by this time, and I didn't think I could
handle the back as well, so I found an opening and
took it. It seemed unusually peaceful in the car.

It was a little early for Sarah Johnson's work
shift, and I remembered I hadn't eaten lunch.
Maybe I'd go early and visit with Archie while I

forced myself to eat another piece of that homemade pie.

Blueberry was on the menu today, a flavor I can never resist. Archie served it up with his usual graciousness. His whites today had the grease stains in different places, so I could assume that he did change clothes occasionally.

"So. Anything new with your investigation?" he asked.

"Not a lot," I admitted. "Jean's death kind of threw a kink in things, didn't it?"

"'Cause you were thinkin' she done it, right?"

I took a big forkful of pie, not wanting to admit he was right.

"Hey, I mighta thought so, too," he chuckled, "if I hadn't of known Jean so well. She had a temper. Man, that woman could really let you have it. Well, I mean she never let *me* have the temper, but I've seen her tie into these girls here sometimes."

He glanced up the counter, making sure the other customers weren't listening.

"One night, ol' Gary come by. He was raggin' on her about something, and pow! She let him have it. No way did she take any stuff off that husband of hers."

"But you still didn't think she killed him?"

"Naw. No way. Jean had a quick temper. You pissed her off, she let fly. Whew! The language got pretty hot sometimes. But then it was done. Just that quick. Jean never held nothin' inside. Five minutes later she'd have her arm around you, makin' up. I don't think she had it in her to plan something out, wait around, and strike. Not Jean."

He resumed filling the salt shakers while I finished off the pie. It was a quarter to four, and I decided to wait out in the parking lot for Sarah. Whatever she had to say, she might not want to say it in front of Archie. I put some money beside my empty plate and waved at him down at the other end of the counter.

Sarah's old pickup truck zipped into the lot at one minute to four. Luckily, this time I was safely in my own vehicle, not crossing the lot.

"Hi, Sarah." I approached quickly, wanting to catch her before she went inside. "I got your message, but no one answered your phone."

She seemed breathless and rushed. "Oh, yeah," she answered vaguely.

"Look, if you don't have time now, we can talk later. Want me to call you tomorrow?"

She searched mentally to remember why she'd called. "Yeah, that would be better," she said. "Oh, wait, now I know. I just wanted to ask if the police have released Jean's car yet. I loaned her a paperback book, and she'd told me it was out in the car. Then we got busy and I forgot about it. It's no big thing but I would like to get it back sometime."

I hadn't realized that the police had impounded the car. But then, it wasn't at the house, so I guess it made sense.

"Why would they take her car?" I asked.

Sarah was fast-walking toward the back entrance of the diner. I trotted to keep pace.

She stopped and looked puzzled. "Oh, didn't I tell you? The night she was killed, she and I got off work at the same time. We walked out together. There were no other cars in the lot and no one standing around. I was in a hurry so I jumped in my truck and took off." She looked at me with eyes so full of guilt it made me want to cry. "Usually we look out for each other. Make sure both our cars start, you know, just being careful. But that night, I left. And there must have been someone waiting for her in her car."

A chill ran up from the base of my spine to my neck and down both arms.

19

"Why didn't you tell me Jean was killed in the car?" I wasn't actually yelling, but I could feel my vocal chords stretching to reach their current level.

"Now wait just a minute," Kent Taylor responded. "You're not a police officer, not even a licensed private investigator. You just don't have the right to certain information."

"Okay. I know that." Feeling somewhat deflated, I realized I better tread lightly. "It's just that you've arrested Stacy for this and I'm trying to help her."

"I know, Charlie, but did it ever occur to you that maybe you can't help her? Maybe she's guilty? You can't fix the world, Charlie, much as you'd like to.

I'm being pretty tolerant with you as it is."

He was right, of course. But it didn't make me ready to give up.

"Can you tell me whether you found any evidence in the car?"

"No, I can't." Meaning he wouldn't.

"Have you found the murder weapon?"

He shuffled a little as he admitted they hadn't.

"Then you can't definitely prove Stacy did it, can you?"

"You're on thin ice here, Charlie. Better just drop it."

I was, and I did. Besides, it was getting late and I'd about had it after the previous sleepless night. I picked up Rusty from the now-deserted office, went home, microwaved a frozen dinner, and watched the news on TV. That was even more depressing than what I was facing in real life, so I popped a video tape of *Casablanca* into the VCR. Two hours later I was weeping but happy. I went to bed.

I awoke the next morning with the oddest feeling that I was forgetting something vitally important. I looked at the calendar, convinced that I'd missed a tax deadline or dentist appointment but that wasn't it. I poured cereal in a bowl, added milk and couldn't get the nagging feeling out of my mind. Halfway to the office I remembered Gary's papers on my desk at home. I couldn't believe I'd let an entire day pass without checking them out. At the

very next intersection, I made a left, then another,
circling the block. Ten minutes later, I was on the
phone telling Sally that I'd be working from home
this morning.

The wad of papers waited just where I'd left
them. In my haste in the Detweiller bedroom the
other day, I hadn't taken time to unfold or
straighten them all. I'd picked out most of the old
newspapers and racing forms, leaving them behind,
but these notes were in their original state. It was
an assortment of notebook pages, cocktail napkins,
and scribbled-on business cards. I carried the whole
mess to the kitchen table and made myself a cup of
tea for fortification.

Carefully, I unfolded and flattened each sheet.
At first, there was no way to categorize them. I
simply laid each new item out until the table top was
covered. I had no idea what to look for but I tried to
keep an open mind. Blackmail material, IOUs, dirty
pictures — I'd take whatever I could get. Unfortunately, there was nothing quite that obvious. Most
of the scraps appeared to contain bets. Little scrib-
bled notes where someone down at Penguin's had
told Gary to place a bet for him. I began stacking
those in one pile.

I spread the business cards out like some kind
of solitaire game. Many of them were Gary's own
cards, Detweiller Enterprises, with notes written on
the backs. Others belonged to an interesting variety

of people. Among them, Charles Tompkins, the Tanoan resident in the cold white house who'd been shafted to the tune of twenty thousand dollars. He'd brushed me off when I'd spoken to him, but now I wondered. His name appeared several times, along with some hefty sums of cash and names of race horses. One caught my eye — Bet the Farm. An odd name for an animal. As far as I could tell, Tompkins — Charlie T. as he was referred to in the notes — had wagered fifty thousand on that one. He'd been cavalier about losing twenty thousand, but if his total losses were closer to a hundred, could even he afford that? A few other names on the list were recognizable, including some of our city's sleazier attorneys and politicians. I got the little spiral notebook from my purse and wrote down a list of names, addresses and phone numbers. I had no idea what I'd do with them, but it was handier having them listed in one place than on fifty little bits of paper. Having done that, I debated what to do next. I chewed my pencil, although it's hard on the teeth and not particularly good for the pencil, either.

The big dilemma I was having with all this was in finding Jean's connection to it. It wasn't hard to find dozens of people that might have been cheated or, cheated on, by Gary. But how did Jean's death tie in? The only thing that made sense was that somehow she'd known something about someone. Thinking back to the day I'd visited their bedroom,

I couldn't see that the papers had been disturbed in weeks. I seriously doubted that Jean had gone through them, learned something, confronted that person, and gotten herself killed for it. So, if these papers weren't her information source, what was?

Sitting here chewing a pencil and agonizing over this wasn't solving anything. And it was driving me crazy. I had to *do* something. It was nearly noon. I picked up the phone and dialed Stacy's number. She answered on the second ring.

"Stace, hi. Just thought I'd check in with you."

"Hello, Charlie. I'm fine, thank you." Her tone was stiff enough to starch shirts.

"Stacy? Is everything all right."

"Yes. Just wonderful, thanks." I'd swear the words came out through clenched teeth.

"Is this a bad time?"

"It really is," she replied.

"Do you need help? Should I come over?"

"Not right now. I'll talk to you later." She hung up before I could think of the next thing to say.

I slammed the receiver down, pulled my jacket from the coat rack near the door, and had it halfway on before I stopped to think. She said she didn't need help. In fact, what had she really said? Granted, the conversation was stiff, the call clearly not welcome, but there could be other reasons. Maybe I'd caught them in the middle of great sex. Maybe they were having the reconciliation of a lifetime.

I took a deep breath and shed my jacket. I had to tell myself that Stacy's problems were not mine, thank goodness. She had to work out whatever was going on at home. She'd only hired me to find out who killed Gary Detweiller. So far, I was doing a sorry job of that. I went back into the kitchen and gathered Gary's papers into a bundle. I folded the whole wad and stuffed them back into my purse. I should probably try to find a way to put them back, although I couldn't imagine what Josh would want with them. All his parent's belongings would probably be thrown out when he moved. I wondered if he'd contacted his aunt about moving in with her. On impulse, I dialed his number. The phone rang twelve times but no answer.

I wanted to talk to Josh again, and to Stacy. And then there was Larry Burke. I'd still like to know whether he'd followed me Friday night or if it was someone he knew, or if it was purely random. Both my visits to Penguin's had ended badly. Slashed tire one time, terrorized by a dark truck the other. Seemed like more than coincidence.

In the meantime, since I couldn't reach anyone I wanted to talk to, I decided my only choice was to go to the office and get some regular work done. Maybe I'd try Stacy again later this afternoon.

As it turned out I didn't have to. I'd been at the office a couple of hours, picking through the work on my desk wishing that something in the stack looked

appealing enough to do. Sally had left at one, and I
found myself wanting the phone to ring, just so I
wouldn't have to answer letters or worse yet, get
back to my tax returns. I wandered the halls like a
lost waif, making cups of tea, scrounging through
the kitchen drawers for snacks but only coming up
with two vanilla sandwich cookies loosely wrapped
in torn cellophane. They were disgusting to look at
and, after I'd finished the second one, I decided they
really didn't have that much flavor.

By three o'clock I was beginning to feel ridiculous. Why was I here, pretending to work, when my
mind was elsewhere? I felt itchy about the Detweiller murders. The answer had to be here close by
somewhere. I told myself that the police were working on it, but that didn't make me any less anxious
to be out there myself. I left Rusty to help Ron with
the phones and started out to my car.

The weather had turned nasty again, our few
days of spring sunshine gone. A bitter wind drilled
through my jeans, making my legs feel like they
were encased in ice tubing. Clouds hung low,
shrouding the Sandias in gray, obscuring their jag-
ged face. The air smelled moist and the ground was
faintly damp from a five-minute sprinkle that had
passed through. I zipped up my jacket and jogged
toward the Jeep. Inside, the air felt heavy and
warm, a nice contrast to the cutting wind outside. I
let the engine idle while I thought about what to do

next.

My thoughts kept flitting back to the papers I'd looked at this morning, Gary's betting notes. And the name that kept coming back to me was Charles Tompkins. The man had been extremely nervous when I'd approached him the last time. Then he'd brushed off his twenty thousand dollar loss like it was nothing. From Gary's notes it appeared Tompkins had lost a great deal more than twenty grand. The next thing I knew, my Jeep was on I-25, heading north for the San Mateo exit.

The Tanoan guard didn't question me when I said I was going to the Tompkins residence. I wove my way through the winding streets. A tumbleweed that had somehow found its way into the neighborhood rolled across the road in front of me. I felt pretty sure that weeds weren't allowed here but I slowed down for it anyway.

Charles Tompkins' house showed no signs of life. I pulled up to the curb and stared at it for a couple of minutes. All three garage doors were closed and all the windows wore a blank look, hidden behind white sheer drapes. It wasn't even four o'clock yet, I realized, a little early for the over-achievers to be home from the office. I debated whether to wait around or try again later. Curiosity got the better of me. Watching how the rich folks conduct themselves might prove entertaining.

I cruised past Stacy's house. It, too, stood like a

large empty-faced mammoth. Brad's Mercedes waited in the driveway though, so I decided not to stop for a chat. Whatever was going on behind their closed doors right now wasn't something I wanted to get involved in. Around the neighborhood, cars were beginning to arrive — executives who allowed themselves to come home early, teens out of school who drove better cars than mine. I wondered what these kids would strive for in their lifetimes. They already had so much, all handed to them by virtue of the fact that they were born when and where they were. Would they grow up to want even more, or would they languish into do-nothingness, never having done anything for themselves. I pictured a lot of lost souls here.

Back at Tompkins' place a car now stood in the drive, almost a junker by these standards, a Ford Thunderbird that must have been at least three years old. Charles Tompkins himself was just stepping out of the car. He wore a dark business suit and conservative tie. He balanced a briefcase and cellular telephone while reaching for a plastic sheathed garment from the cleaners and trying to lock the car door at the same time. I parked by the curb and walked toward him. I'd reached the rear of the car before he noticed me.

"Hi. Charlie Parker," I reminded him.

He gave me a puzzled look over the top of the briefcase.

"I'm investigating the Gary Detweiller case."

"Oh, yes." His tone was noncommittal, his face closed and guarded.

"Could I talk to you again for a minute?"

I could tell he didn't want to talk, and he especially didn't want to invite me inside. But the wind was ferocious now, even stronger here near the foothills than it had been in the valley. His cleaning bag was whipping around like an unruly pet trying to get away. He hesitated a minute, then ungraciously invited me in.

It was almost comical to watch him juggle his many burdens while trying to open the front door and disarm the alarm system. He positioned his body between me and the keypad so I couldn't see what code numbers he punched in. Having a lot of possessions certainly breeds paranoia.

"Excuse me a minute," he said. He disappeared into a room off the den, leaving me standing in the white entry hall.

The white and chrome living room waited, silent and unoccupied. Undisturbed vacuum cleaner tracks made neat white paths in a perfectly symmetrical pattern. On my right, a formal dining room had the same freshly cleaned look. The almost invisible table had chrome legs and a heavy glass top. In the exact center stood a glossy black bowl filled with spiky black twigs. Some decorator had probably charged him a fortune for the thing. Beyond the

table, an all-glass hutch held a set of shiny black
dishes. They stood out like large bullseyes in contrast to the white walls, white carpet, and non-color
of the rest of the house. I wondered what it would
feel like to pull out a slingshot and ping them from
their colorless perch.

"Now, what can I do for you?"

Tompkins' voice startled me, caught in the act
of mentally vandalizing his dining room. He had
loosened the knot in his tie and unbuttoned the top
button of his gray-striped white shirt. He had
dumped all the excess baggage he'd carried in with
him. His fingers combed through his mass of curly
blond hair, trying to restore order to the mess the
wind had made.

"I just wondered whether there was anything
more to your association with Gary Detweiller that
you might not have mentioned to me the other day."

Something flickered in his eyes, something so
fleeting that it was gone in a fraction of a second. A
tiny pucker showed on his upper lip but that, too,
disappeared instantly.

"I don't believe I've thought of any other information," he said.

"Not even the name of a race horse you lost
heavily on," I prodded. "A horse named Bet the
Farm."

His thin lips pursed together noticeably this
time. "I'm not sure what business this is of yours,"

he said tersely.

"Truthfully, it probably isn't any of my business, except that you grossly underestimated your losses to Detweiller. Except that a hundred thousand dollars might be a lot stronger motive for murder than a mere twenty. And except that our client is still on the hook for something she didn't do." I stopped, realizing that I'd said a lot more than I intended, a lot more than was probably smart.

Suddenly the house felt very lonely and very quiet. I realized that, although these homes might be packed together like sardines, the neighbors probably weren't home. I felt a hollow sensation low in my stomach.

Tompkins' mouth twitched in a half-smile.

"How'd you find out about the other losses?" he asked.

"Gary kept very thorough records," I told him, keeping my voice flat.

"He did, hunh?" he said. He turned toward the den, pulling off his tie as he went. I followed without speaking. He chose a glass off the shelf above the bar and reached below for ice cubes from an ice maker built into the cabinets.

"I should have known this would come down to some kind of blackmail scheme." He filled the glass half full of whiskey and took a long swallow before speaking again.

"Blackmail? Excuse me?"

"Just come out with it. What is it you want?"

"I just want some answers. I don't personally care whether you lost a million bucks to the guy. Your finances are your own problem. I'm just trying to find out who killed Gary Detweiller."

"Well, I sure as hell didn't." He downed the rest of the drink and poured another.

"Where were you Wednesday night a week ago?"

He chuckled. "You sound like a little skinny Perry Mason."

I stood my ground. Skinny?

"Actually, I was out of town all week. At a banking convention in Atlanta. You can have that verified through my office, the hotel, and about two hundred other people who heard me give the key-note speech."

"Blackmail? I don't get it."

He set the glass down and leaned against the bar, perching his butt against the edge of the counter top, arms folded across his chest.

"My ex-wife. Or I should say, soon-to-be-ex. She's got people practically digging into my under-wear drawer to find hidden assets. I assumed you were working for them."

"I told you what I was looking for, right up front," I said.

He gave me a look that basically said, Get real. "Do you think her investigators are going to come out with the real questions?"

Well, okay, probably not. I didn't say it. I left a couple of minutes later, feeling a little sheepish. Until I got into the car and thought about it. Tompkins was a cool one. He had been careful to steer the conversation away from Gary, away from their dealings. I didn't care what he said, though. A hundred thousand dollar loss doesn't come easy to anyone. And a hundred thousand is plenty of reason for murder.

20

I cruised past Stacy's house once more on my way out of the neighborhood. Brad's car was still in the driveway so I didn't stop. Three blocks away, I spotted a pizza place on the corner. I realized I was famished. It was still early enough that I found a parking place right by the door. Almost ordained, it seemed.

They sold pizza by the slice. I ordered one with mushrooms and black olives and a Greek salad. I found a table in a deserted corner and waited there, crunching on the salad. Out of curiosity I pulled the sheaf of papers from my purse again. I hadn't organized them, and it took a few minutes to locate Charles Tompkins' name among the scraps of scrawlings.

I heard my name being called so I got up to collect my pizza slice. Back at the table, one of the racing forms almost jumped out at me. Why hadn't I noticed this before? Tompkins hadn't lost money on Bet the Farm. The horse had won. I remembered Tompkins' comment about hidden assets.

The horse had won, and maybe Gary hadn't paid off. Gary had written dates beside some of his hand-written entries, including Tompkins' big wager on Bet the Farm. I pulled out my checkbook calendar to verify the date. He'd placed the bet two days before Stacy had hired me to locate her missing watch. Could it be pure coincidence, or did Gary have an urgent reason to get out of town? Like maybe a hundred thousand reasons that someone might be angry with him?

Tompkins wouldn't have pulled the trigger. How stupid could I be? The way he'd done it was perfect. Out of town at a week-long convention, hundreds of witnesses as to his whereabouts, a hired assassin to get rid of Detweiler. The sheet of paper suddenly felt hot in my hand. I laid it down, staring at Gary's long, slanted writing as I finished my pizza. I remembered Ron's caution to me about withholding evidence. The police needed to know about this. I still couldn't figure out the connection between Tompkins and Jean Detweiller. That puzzle would take some work. But I didn't see how Kent

Taylor could ignore this new finding. Surely, he would have to admit that Stacy was no longer the only suspect. I stuffed the last bite of pizza into my mouth and walked out of the place, still chewing.

It was one minute to five when I pulled into the only parking spot I could find within three blocks of the downtown police station. I had a feeling Taylor worked from eight to five and might already be gone by now. I locked my car and pushed my way up the crowded sidewalk.

Taylor sat at his desk with stacks of file folders surrounding him. He was making notes in one, resting his forehead on the other hand. Gone was the freshly pressed look he usually wore in the mornings. The precisely knotted tie hung over his chair and his hair looked like it had been the victim of an eggbeater attack.

He seemed completely unaware of my presence. I ahummed a couple of times before he looked up.

"Charlie."

I ignored the unspoken, What do you want? He went back to his writing. Helping myself to an extra chair, I pulled it to the front of his desk and sat still with my hands in my lap like a nice, polite little girl. It almost killed me.

He made a few more notes in his file, then closed the cover.

"Now, I assume by the way you're twitching in your chair that you came here to tell me something urgent," he said.

"I've found another suspect in the Detweiler case that had as much reason to kill Detweiler as anyone. More reason than Stacy did." I outlined the basics for him.

"That's crazy, Charlie. A guy bets on a horse and wins, he doesn't kill the bookie."

"He might if the bookie left town with the guy's winnings. Picture this — Tompkins places a large bet on Friday. Gets the word Saturday that he'd won. He's ready to collect, but Gary's gone. Out of town, can't be located. Tompkins spends the next three days getting madder and madder, until finally he's ready to kill Gary. He's also had time to think about it and decides he shouldn't do it himself. So he hires help."

"Or maybe he just couldn't take time out of his busy schedule to sit for an evening in Detweiler's driveway," he replied sarcastically.

"Come on, Kent, you have to admit this is at least as strong a motive as Stacy's."

He cocked his head to one side, almost but not quite agreeing.

"At least look into it," I asked.

I could tell by the look on his face that he had really wanted to close this file with Stacy's name on the bottom line. I had managed to complicate his life once again in the last ten minutes and he wasn't crazy about it. I left the station without knowing what, if anything, he'd do with the information.

Traffic was heavy as I left the downtown area. I managed to catch every red light. There was nothing to do but fall in with the slow pace of all the other vehicles. It was nearly six when I reached the office, but Ron's light was still on.

Rusty greeted me at the door like I'd been gone for days. After quite a bit of hand licking and sniffing my pockets for misplaced cheeseburgers, he let me go upstairs.

Ron was at his desk still, phone in hand. I thought the wrinkles were a little more noticeable around his eyes, and his thin hair was stuck to the top of his bald spot.

"Rough day?" I asked.

"Just a long one," he replied. "The usual."

"How about an enchilada dinner? My treat."

He pulled himself out of his chair, groaning slightly as he stood. He's only six years older than I, making me wonder if this was the kind of shape I'd be in before long. He reached for his Stetson on the wall rack. We checked the doors and windows and boarded our respective cars for the drive to Pedro's. Somehow, tonight I was eager for that margarita.

Pedro had the drinks plus a bowl of salsa and a basket of chips on the table almost before we sat down. If it weren't for Concha, I could probably fall in love with this man.

"How's your case going?" Ron asked after the first salty sip from his glass.

I told him of today's discoveries.

"At least I think the police will have to investigate the possibility that Stacy isn't the only suspect in this case," I told him. "I just wish I had a better idea of how Jean's murder tied in to all this. I still haven't figured out why anyone would have killed her. And it has to be related. She was shot with the same gun."

"You think Tompkins paid a hit man to do Gary? Well, the same guy could have killed Jean, not knowing about the relationship."

"Just for the fun of it, you mean? I doubt that." The conversation was becoming ridiculous. "I guess I'll leave that part to the police. At least I can tell Stacy that there is another suspect."

The enchiladas arrived just then and we stayed busy shoveling steaming tortilla, chicken, cheese, and green chile into ourselves. Rusty helped with the fallen chips. Twenty minutes later I was full, but managed to put away a honey-filled yeasty sopapilla for dessert.

We visited with Pedro and Concha for a few minutes before leaving. At home, I felt restless. I wanted to call Stacy but found myself putting it off, telling myself that it was already getting late. The truth was, I didn't want to talk to Brad or to have him around when I spoke with her. And I really wasn't sure why. Just that contact with him was something I dreaded a little more each time it happened.

I puttered around the house, finding little things to keep myself busy until eleven. I went to bed then, more out of habit than from tiredness. Despite efforts to get comfortable, my eyes stared wide awake at the ceiling for a long time. I couldn't rid myself of the feeling that there was more to the story than I'd discovered so far.

I fell into an uneasy sleep, where I dreamed that someone slashed all four of my tires while the Jeep was parked at the Tanoan Country Club. Tangled images of jacks and tow trucks and a maitre d' who feigned concern over my plight filled the night. I awoke abruptly, relieved that I no longer had to deal with the problem.

It was early morning, the room defined in colorless shades of gray and black. I rolled toward the night table. The red numerals on my clock radio provided the only spot of color in the room. Five-fourteen, they said. I groaned and rolled away from them, but my adrenaline was already pumping too hard for sleep to return.

Ideas boinged around inside my skull, giving me no peace. The dream of more flat tires only reminded me that here was another aspect of the mystery that I had yet failed to solve. In my mind, I had linked Larry Burke with that incident as well as with the dark truck that followed me home. But I had no proof. And the only way I'd get proof was either to confront him or to return to Penguin's and try to get some evidence. Neither option appealed to me at the moment.

Thirty minutes later, I was still staring at the clock, still no closer to drifting back to sleep. I was also mentally kicking myself because I couldn't seem to get motivated to do what I needed to do — visit Larry Burke again.

Mental butt-kicking usually serves to get me in motion, and this time was no exception. By six o'clock I had forced myself into the shower and by six-thirty I was in the predawn traffic, headed across town. I couldn't remember the last time I'd actually used my headlights in the morning.

Judging by the absolute blackness at the Burke house, they weren't much for early mornings either. Fortunately, McDonalds didn't have any such prejudices and I was able to fortify myself with a breakfast thing that combined eggs, sausage and biscuit in a way I'd never seen it done before. This wonderful concoction and a cup of really black coffee would keep me alive until Larry Burke finally showed his face. In the back seat, Rusty just about went into seizures over the egg and sausage smell, so I ordered him one, too. We'd both be watching our cholesterol for days.

I parked in front of the house next to Burke's. I

wanted a clear view of his driveway, but didn't want him getting a clear view of me first. This is tricky. A large juniper at the corner of his property would, I hoped, do the job.

Rusty wolfed down his breakfast treat in approximately five seconds but I knew we ought to ration our provisions. I nibbled at mine, thinking this would make the time pass more quickly. It didn't, but at least I had something to do while I was bored out of my head. Rusty eyed my sandwich and drooled, but I ignored him.

Finally, about seven-thirty a light appeared in what I supposed to be the Burke kitchen. Behind closed mini-blinds I could see a shape move back and forth occasionally, but couldn't tell who it was. At five minutes before eight, Larry emerged, perfectly coifed as usual, spiffy checked jacket hanging just right from his small frame. I sincerely hoped he didn't have to be at work by eight, because he was about to be late.

I met him at the door to his sports car. It was unfortunate that I'd left my camera at home, because the look on his face would have made an interesting shot.

"Hello, Larry."

He was able to close his jaw with some effort. His hands seemed to be oddly restless, reaching first for the car door, then into his pockets, clasping together, then back to the pockets.

"I'm wondering why you're so surprised to see me," I told him.

More fidgeting.

"Could it be that someone was supposed to chase me down Friday night? Maybe I'm not supposed to be walking and talking right now."

His eyes darted toward the front door, then up and down the street. He noticed my car for the first time, where Rusty was quite visibly pressing against the window. A dozen stories flitted through his list of possibilities, but finally he slumped.

"Willie, down at Penguin's, he told me you were trouble," he said. "He wanted to know if he could teach you a lesson."

"What did I ever do to him?" I asked incredulously.

Burke shrugged, like he just realized he didn't know. "Well, not him really — the guy he works for. Somehow you've pi— ticked that guy off."

"What are you talking about? *Who* are you talking about?"

"Some rich dude. Willie works for him, as a security guard, I think. I don't know his name. I've seen him around the club." He was uncomfortable with this. I got the idea that he didn't really know, and that he'd opened his mouth to Willie without knowing enough of the story.

"At least tell me Willie's last name," I insisted.

"I, umm, I don't know it." He stared at his toes

while mumbling the words.

"You don't know Willie. You don't know who he works for. Yet you gave him permission to chase me down, to scare the hell out of me!" I spat the words at him. "You are something else, Burke. I just wish I could find a way to pin Gary's murder on you." I spun and stalked toward my car, leaving him standing in the driveway.

Sitting in my car, I gripped the wheel with both hands. My heart was thumping audibly and my face felt curiously flushed. I breathed deeply while I watched Burke start his own car, race the engine, and zip out of the driveway. I seldom lose my temper. When I do, I hate the physical effects. I reached for my styrofoam cup of coffee. The lid was still tightly in place and the coffee was reasonably warm. The long drag I took soothed my insides.

What next? I was only a couple of blocks from the Detweiller house. Maybe I could catch Josh before he left for school, assuming he was still going to school these days.

21

The sun had finally cleared Sandia Crest, throwing long shadows across the yards. Josh's house faced west, its front yard completely in shadow this early. His primer gray car was alone in the driveway. I pulled in behind it.

The place was quiet. No rock music blasted forth, no sign of activity. I opened the rickety screen and knocked on the door. No response. Once again, a bit firmer. This time Josh answered. He wore only a pair of boxer shorts, dark blue and green tartan plaid. His dark hair was sleep-mussed and his angular face showed a dark shadow at the jaw. His smooth well-muscled body had a disquieting effect on me.

"Sorry, I thought you'd be leaving for school about now," I said.

He said something but since he was rubbing both hands over his sleepy face at the same time the words only mumbled out. He turned away, leaving the front door standing wide open, which I took to mean "Come on in." I stepped into the dim living room.

Jean's housekeeping skills might not have been much, but the absence of a woman was becoming obvious here. The vinyl recliner was piled high with clothes, worn and discarded at random. Plates with dried on food and cutlery stuck to the surfaces waited in odd places around the room — on the sofa, the end tables, the TV set. A heap of school books sat at one end of the sofa, with a pillow and two coats thrown on top. Obviously, the books had not been used in days.

Josh emerged from his room, zipping on a pair of jeans. He hadn't got around to finding a shirt yet. He combed his hair by running all ten fingers through it, front to back in one swipe.

"Can I get you some breakfast?" I asked.

"Uh, sure, if there's anything in the house." He glanced around like a bowl of cereal might show up just about anywhere.

I shed my jacket and purse behind the recliner and gathered up the crusty remains of previous meals on my way to the kitchen. Obviously, Josh had not spent lots of time in here. The kitchen was far neater than the living room. The plate I'd used on my last visit here was still in the sink, soaking with the same water I'd run there. The trash can overflowed with sacks and wrappers from fast food places.

"You got any cereal, milk, stuff like that?" I called toward the other room.

He appeared in the doorway, shrugging.

"Well, let's look." The date on the milk carton had expired two days ago but it smelled passable. I found a box of Froot Loops and a clean bowl. Clearing a spot at the kitchen table, I set the cereal down for him. He grinned as I poured the milk for him.

"So, what's going on?" I asked.

"Not much," he mumbled with red and yellow loops poking out between his lips.

"You talked to your aunt?"

He nodded. Despite my attempt to sit with him and carry on conversation, I couldn't look at the dirty dishes while doing nothing. He didn't strike me as the type who would be touchy about someone else stepping in and cleaning up. I set the stopper, squirted dish soap into the sink and started the hot water spraying over the dishes. Josh crunched down the cereal quickly and refilled the bowl.

"So, are you going to be moving in with her?" I asked as I poked around under the sink, looking for trash bags.

"She wants me to come Saturday." His eyes narrowed belligerently. "I ain't going, man."

"What did you find out about school?"

"She's checking on that. Says she thinks I can probably stay at Highland."

I dumped the contents of the trash can into a plastic bag and tied the top in a knot. "Have you been attending?"

"Some."

"At the risk of sounding like a social worker, Josh, you can't afford to let your work fall behind. You've always been a good student, haven't you?"

"I guess." He shrugged again and turned back to his cereal.

I cruised through the house, finding several more dishes and a few glasses tucked away in odd spots. I returned them to the kitchen, adding them to the sudsy water in the sink. The dish sponge had dried to a disk about the thickness of cardboard but it sprang to life again when it hit the hot water. I began the routine of washing, rinsing and stacking.

Josh tipped his bowl up to his mouth and drank the milk from it. He started to leave the kitchen but remembered to pick up the dishes he'd just used and slip them into the sink for me.

"Look," he said, "you don't have to do that. I was going to clean up today."

"It's okay. It'll go faster if I pitch in."

He gave me one of those lopsided Elvis grins.

"Why don't you take that trash out, then maybe get another bag and gather up all those old newspapers and stuff in the other room," I suggested after he'd stood uncertainly in the doorway for several minutes.

He grinned again and went willingly to the tasks. He might look grownup, but there was still a kid inside. I finished the dishes, wiped the counter and table, and tidied up the rest of the kitchen. When I went into the living room, Josh was stuffing newspapers and junk mail, one piece at a time, into a trash bag.

"Make sure you check that mail before you toss it," I reminded. "There might be bills and important things in there."

He looked up at me, like he'd never considered the possibility. I circled the room, gathering castoff clothing in my arms.

"Do you have a washer and dryer?" I asked.

"I think Mom went to the Laundromat," he said, as if he weren't quite certain.

"Okay, where's the clothes basket?" At his blank look, I told him I'd find it myself.

No sign of a basket in the bathroom, but while in there I couldn't resist wiping off the sink and straightening the shampoo bottles in the tub. I wasn't going to scrub toilets for this kid but I do have this tidy streak that can't abide clutter. I put away the toothpaste tube and his toothbrush almost without thinking.

I located the laundry basket on the floor of Jean's closet. Two bras and panties lay in the bottom of it. I took them out, thinking to spare Josh the vivid reminders. I carried the empty basket back to the living room and dumped the heap of dirties into it. The place was beginning to look almost habitable.

"You'll have quite a job here, moving all this stuff," I commented. "Does your aunt have room for all of it?"

"I don't know," he said shortly. "Guess it'll have to go in storage. The furniture came with the house. But there's all my stuff."

"You want some help packing? I could come by this afternoon," I suggested. "Help you pack boxes. It would be less work for your aunt when she comes."

"Yeah. Whatever." He probably had not considered the work involved in moving. He was still acting like the move wouldn't happen.

I glanced at my watch. It was almost nine.

"Look, Josh, I really think you ought to be in school. Here, take this laundry basket with you. You can stop at the Laundromat after school and do these."

He didn't look thrilled, but he didn't argue. We walked out together, he with his arms loaded with books, me carrying the laundry. I set the basket on the front passenger seat of his car so he couldn't ignore it.

Rusty had sacked out on the back seat of the Jeep and he barely raised his head to acknowledge that I'd returned. I backed out of the driveway so Josh could leave, but I hung back slightly to make sure he did.

As I drove across town toward the office, I thought back to Larry Burke's odd admission this morning. Why would Willie, his friend from Penguin's, want to frighten me off this case? I felt certain that Willie had also been responsible for my slashed tire the first time I'd been there. But, why? Larry had mentioned that Willie worked for a man Larry had seen a few times around the club. Did he mean Tanoan Country Club? I thought of Charles Tompkins. He was the only Tanoan person I could think of who'd been deeply involved with Detweiller. Other than Stacy.

I spent the rest of the day at the office, tending to small undone tasks, mostly brooding over the deadlock I felt about the case. Ron was out for the day, leaving me no one to bounce ideas off. For some reason, I felt a certain sense of dread, like something was about to happen but I couldn't figure out what.

At five o'clock I dialed Josh Detweiller's number. He answered on the second ring.

"Hey, Josh. It's Charlie. You ready for some help with the packing?"

"Sure." I ignored the sullen tone. Who could blame him? His whole life was changing rapidly.

"I'll bring dinner," I offered. "McDonald's or Burger King?"

He wanted a Whopper with cheese, leave off the "salad," as he called all the trimmings, large fries, large Dr. Pepper. I felt like an employee by the time I finished taking his order.

It was getting dark when I arrived at Josh's. I had taken Rusty home and fed him. Figuring it might be late by the time I got back home, I left lights on for myself. I stopped for the burgers and pulled into Josh's driveway soon after.

We put first things first, heading for the kitchen table to eat. Josh was uncommunicative through dinner, shoving the burger and fries into his mouth almost non-stop. I couldn't think of a lot to say, either. He finished his dinner first and went into his room. I threw away the wrappers from the food, then went out to the Jeep to get the packing boxes I'd rounded up earlier.

Josh's room looked like what I imagined every teenager's room must look like. Clothing was strewn on nearly every surface. Clean or dirty, I couldn't tell. The basket of laundry from this morning was in the living room, presumably clean although everything had been mashed down into permanent wrinkles. I assumed the articles I saw here were dirty — I just couldn't figure out how a person could manage so much in one short day. The walls had been painted black (the landlord would love this) and the windows were covered in heavy blackout shades. A blue neon fixture, twisted into words of some unknown language, cast extremely dim light in one corner. Another, red neon this time, gave the rest of the room a purple cast and made our faces look sickly. Black sheets on the bed were twisted into knotted heaps. This is probably an admission of age, but I have to confess that I don't remember being this messy myself. Given my present penchant for obsessive neatness, I'm *sure* my room never looked this way.

"Is there another light in here?" I asked, flipping the wall switch futilely.

"Nah, I took the bulbs out of that one," he said, lifting his chin upward to indicate the empty ceiling fixture. "Couldn't stand my mom blasting me with bright light every time she walked in the room."

"Can you see·well enough to work in here?" Even as I said it, I heard echoes of my own mother's voice reminding me to turn on more light. "Never mind. I'll start packing things in the other bedroom if you want to work on this."

He halfheartedly dropped a wadded up t-shirt into one of the packing boxes. I walked into Gary and Jean's former bedroom, unsure where to start. It felt like a severe invasion of privacy to paw through their belongings. Especially since I'd already done it once when searching for Gary's papers. I ended up leaving the dresser drawers intact, thinking the aunt could decide what to do with their clothing. I cleared the surfaces of the furniture, packing clock radio, books, and small personal items. Everything barely filled one box. I stripped and folded the bedding, placing it in a neat stack at the foot of the bed. I'd been at this for probably an hour and decided I should check on Josh's progress.

Noise from the living room sent me in that direction, only to find Josh on the couch with the TV on and an open beer in hand.

"Finished already?" I really tried not to sound sarcastic.

He ignored me until I ahummed.

"I said I ain't goin'" he reminded me.

"Would you rather I work on the kitchen or your room?" I asked.

His eyes went back to the television and he took a long pull on the beer. The thought went through my mind that this probably wasn't his first of the evening. The personality change from the good-natured young man I'd poured cereal for this morning was just too marked.

The kitchen cupboards were a simple matter. The Detweiller's hadn't owned much. If they once had fancy china and wedding silver, it wasn't here now. A four-place-setting set of cheap stoneware and a few assorted cups and bowls, many of which looked like former housing for whipped cream and butter, were the main vessels. I set each item in a box, placing newspaper between, but leaving the boxes open so Josh or his aunt could find whatever they needed. I opened the refrigerator and quickly made up my mind that some things are beyond my charitable kindness. The aunt could handle this.

My watch said it was not quite nine. I had made some progress, and wasn't too tired yet, so I glanced back at Josh's room. Maybe he'd quit because the job was too daunting. He was still in front of the television, with some shoot-em-up movie blasting forth, the f-word in generous use. Not network programming, I gathered. Josh had wandered into the kitchen for more beer at least twice while I worked in there, so I figured it was useless getting him into action now. Without asking, I stepped into his room once more. Maybe if I picked up the first two or three layers and made the bed, it wouldn't look so frightening. He could then finish it tomorrow.

Josh had thrown half a dozen articles of clothing into one of the packing boxes before he gave up. I glanced at them. They lay in inert little heaps, indistinguishable lumps. Gingerly, I reached in and pulled out one of them. This was no way to pack clothes. I folded the t-shirt neatly, then the next and the next. We'd get a lot more into the box if they were flat. Making my way around the room, I soon had all the loose clothing in two boxes. The top of what I presumed to be a desk was littered with junk — pencils, loose change, a lighter, and wads of papers covered the surface. I attempted to stack the papers and decided maybe I could just push the rest of it into a drawer. This is not my usual style but this was not my room, either.

I started to open the top drawer of the desk but it jammed. Something was wedged at an angle near the back of the drawer, keeping it from opening more than about three inches. I could have probably scooped the small junk into the opening and closed it but that went against my grain. I snaked my hand through the opening, feeling blindly for the obstacle and hoping like hell it wouldn't bite.

Whatever the obstruction, it was wedged very well. It felt like something solid and heavy. I pushed at it a few times with no success. Finally, I got my fingers to the bottom of the cluttered drawer and pressed hard at the base of the offending object. It fell with startling suddenness, smashing my middle finger in the process.

"Ouch!" I couldn't help it. The drawer slid open easily now, my injured finger popping straight to my mouth. It wasn't cut, at least I couldn't see any blood in the eerie purple light. I held on to the damaged part for a couple of minutes until the pain subsided. When I reached for the drawer, with my other hand this time, it slid easily open. I was just about to scoop the entire pile of junk from the top of the desk into the drawer when I realized what had hit me. About two-thirds of the way back, not hidden in any way, lay a gun.

It was a black shadow of a thing, and had it not been for the damage to my finger, I would have believed it to be a toy. As it was, I blinked twice just to confirm what I was seeing in the dimly lit room. I reached toward it automatically, but my hand drew back just inches away from it. In that moment I knew, just as sure as I knew my own name or my birthdate, that this was the gun that had killed Gary and Jean.

A crumpled paper napkin lay among the detritus on the desk. I used it to pick up the weapon. It was heavier than I'd expected, once I had the full weight of it in hand. I raised it slowly and sniffed at it. It smelled very faintly like fireworks — like the air smells late in the evening on the Fourth of July. I don't know much about guns, but somehow this told me it had been fired.

The noise from the television set in the living room intruded upon my consciousness again. The hair on my arms prickled suddenly. I turned to find Josh Detweiller standing in the doorway.

22

For a crazy moment I thought he might just give me one of those Elvis smiles. He would come into the room and pick up a magazine. I'd slip the gun back into the drawer unnoticed, then bid him goodnight and get the hell out of there.

It almost worked that way. He stood there watching me for an eternity. Probably about a minute and a half, in reality. I lowered the gun, hoping to put it back where I'd found it. I fumbled for the drawer, unwilling to take my eyes off him. My shaking hand couldn't find it and I backed up. My rear end touched the open drawer. It slid quickly closed, causing me to momentarily lose balance.

Josh was at my side instantly. He reached for

the weapon with shaky hands and I gave it up. For the first time in my life, I wished I'd listened to Ron's advice about guns. At least I'd know whether it was loaded, whether the safety was on or not. It was a little late now for those kinds of wishes.

"What made you do it, Josh?" Now I could only hope to stall long enough to work out a way to get myself out of this alive.

He shrugged, backing away enough to aim the gun at me. His hands weren't shaking now. His lids were half closed, the dark eyes almost sexy looking. I'd never seen him like this before, but then I'd never seen him after several beers, a violent movie, and with a gun in his hand.

My question still hung in the air. He hadn't ignored it, he was contemplating his answer.

"They were mean to me," he finally said.

"Mean to you?" Mean to you! Is that the answer nowadays? Anytime someone is mean to you, you blow them away?

"My old man used to throw me around. Every time he came home drunk, he'd take it out on me and Mom."

"And your mom? Why did she deserve it?" Or had her big mistake been reaching into that drawer the same way I had?

He laughed, an abrupt chuckle that came out as a snort. "She was no better. Whenever Dad hit me, she'd jump in and pull him away. But when he wasn't around, she'd scream at me, call me stupid, and lazy. She was no different than him."

"And so you're gonna solve it the same way they solved everything. Somebody makes you mad, so you just get violent."

He shrugged again. "They deserved it."

The cold attitude chilled me. I rubbed my goose-pimpled arms.

"What about me?" I asked. "Now you feel you have to get rid of me, too?"

"You haven't ever been mean to me, Charlie," he said. He seemed genuinely puzzled about my re-mark.

"What about the police, Josh? Sooner or later they'll figure this out." I was careful not to say that I'd tell them.

"I'll get a good lawyer," he said.

So that's what it boiled down to. A good lawyer could find some kind of defense for Josh. It made me furious but I had no doubt of its feasibility. *Good* lawyers get guilty people off the hook all the time. Right and wrong have ceased to matter. It only matters how good your lawyer is.

"Josh, think about this. You need help, counsel-ing. Let's try to figure out a way."

He stiffened. For the first time since he'd taken the gun from me, I saw anger. It was a cold, unprin-cipled anger.

"I need to think about this," he growled. "Not

with you. Just me, by myself."

He jammed the gun into the waistband of his jeans and, almost in the same move, grabbed a length of nylon climbing rope from the dresser near the door.

"Sit down," he ordered. With his left hand he yanked the chair away from the desk, flinging a bath towel off it. The cord was still in his right hand.

I stared at the gun in his waistband. If I moved quickly, I could probably grab it. What good would that do? I didn't know how to use it. But he didn't know that. I hesitated a second too long. Josh grabbed my shoulder, squeezing it painfully in a grip that brought me to the chair without much effort. He looped the rope around my left wrist, cinching it tight. My right arm was curiously useless, numb from the pressure he'd applied to my collarbone. Before I managed to shake off the feeling, he'd snagged that wrist, too, and was proceeding to wind the rope through the lower chair rungs, effectively pinning my hands down near my ankles in a position that would very soon send my lower back into spasms.

"Ow, Josh, that hurts!"

Oddly enough, he listened. He let a little slack in the rope. A curious kindness from a two-time murderer. He progressed to my ankles, tying them now to the chair legs. At least I had some protection there from my socks.

"Josh, what are you going to do?" I worked to keep the tremor out of my voice.

He yanked at the final knot. "I don't know. I just gotta get out of here. I ain't living with that aunt, and I ain't going to jail. I just gotta figure it out."

I sat still, wondering what he meant to do. He didn't seem to know either. His eyes darted around the room, like he was figuring out what to take with him. He settled on a lightweight jacket and four CDs from the rack beside his stereo. The gun was still in his waistband.

He darted out of my sight, which wasn't difficult since my back was to the door, my eyes aimed at the floor. I strained to hear what was going on. Blaring music from the television in the living room effectively obliterated other sounds. Some bumping noises came from the direction of the kitchen. I twisted to one side then the other, hoping to get some idea. In the macabre black room, I could only see the purplish glow from the two neon lamps. My ears listened for any sound from Josh.

After ten minutes or so, I felt sure he'd really gone. I managed to get enough weight onto my feet that I could lift the chair legs an inch or two off the floor. By hefting my weight at the same time, I managed to turn a few inches to the right. I did this twice, then listened for reprisals from the other rooms. Nothing.

I clumped the chair around enough to see the

doorway into the hall. I was breathing hard from the effort and my lower back was killing me. I saw no sign of Josh. Flickering light from the TV set gave the hall a strobe effect. Between that and the neons I was beginning to feel nauseated. Sitting bent over at the waist wasn't helping, either. I scanned the little bit I could see and found no evidence of Josh. I clumped the chair again, loudly, to see if I'd get a reaction.

Nothing.

Every part of my body hurt. My stomach was doing flip-flops while my arms felt stretched to the breaking point and my collarbone still ached from his ferocious pinch. And all the time I had to think about getting out. There was no doubt in my mind that Josh would be back. It was only a question of how long he'd stay away.

I tried to think where I'd seen the telephone. There was one on the kitchen wall near the door to the hall. If I cranked my neck far enough back, I could even see it. In my present position, it was a good two feet above my head. And with my arms strapped down to the chair rungs, there was no way I'd ever be able to dial it. Think, Charlie. There had been an extension in the master bedroom. The phone had been on the floor near the bed. I had set it up on the nightstand, now conveniently out of my reach. Well, it was my only hope now.

Since I hadn't heard any repercussions from my

earlier movements, I decided it was time to go for it. It couldn't get much more awkward than this, my ankles tied to the chair legs, hands bound beside them. With a little effort, I worked out a system of shifting my weight to my feet, then to the chair. I scooted along like this, like a severely crippled inch-worm. The clutter all over Josh's room didn't help, either. I barrelled over some of the obstacles, kicked others out of my way with the tips of my toes. I had to stop for a breather when I reached the hall, but I knew I couldn't afford to make it a long one.

The hall looked impossibly long. In fact, it was probably less than eight feet to the master bedroom. Then to traverse that room, too . . . I resolved not to think about it. It seemed like a day later that I reached the nightstand, although it had probably been closer to twenty minutes. I had lost all track of time and my watch was cocked around to the far side of my wrist, impossible to see. The phone stood on the nightstand, just as I'd left it, about level with my forehead when I stretched my neck as far as I could. My spirits took a dive. There was no way I could lift the receiver and press the numbers.

Dammit! I hurt all over and knew that Josh might return any time. In a fit of frustration, I reared the chair back on its hind legs and kicked forward with all my might. The nightstand fell sideways and the phone with it. All right!

I scooted over to the phone, which lay upside

down on the rug, the receiver splayed out to the end of its spiral cord. I righted the instrument with my toe and jerked myself into a position where my fingers could touch it. Carefully, I pressed 911.

The receiver was two feet away. I clumped over to it and touched it with my fingers. No way I could raise it to my mouth. I waited until I thought I heard a voice at the other end. With the television still blaring in the background, it was impossible to tell. I shouted toward the mouthpiece, hoping whoever waited out there would be able to understand what I was about to say.

"Get Detective Kent Taylor," I yelled. "Tell him Josh Detweiller is the killer. He's out driving around." I gave a description of the car, berating myself that I'd not troubled to memorize the license number. "Then send someone here to untie me," I shouted. I gave the address, and hoped they got it all. I heard a voice at the other end but couldn't make out the words. My voice was hoarse and I wanted to cry from the pain and frustration. And then I heard the distinct sound of the front door closing.

23

"What are you *doing*?" Josh shouted, taking in the broken nightstand and the phone sprawled across the carpet. He rushed toward me. I expected to be shot or slammed with the butt of the gun at any second.

At that moment I felt curiously detached, as if I were watching the scene being played out in a movie. Somewhere inside, I knew I should be afraid but I'd put the emotion on hold. Instead, I noticed details. No sign of the gun on Josh. What had he done with it? Had he ditched it somewhere in an effort to hide his crimes, or was it simply tucked away in the back of his jeans?

"Josh, this position is killing me," I wailed. "I

need someone to untie me." A sob escaped, a fine bit of acting, I thought.

Seeing me get emotional confused him.

"I didn't mean to hurt you, Charlie," he said, almost kindly. I wondered if the booze was wearing off or if he was having second thoughts about getting me involved.

"Could you just untie my hands? I can't stay bent over like this."

He bent to work on the cords around my left hand. I could see that the gun wasn't in his waistband. His not having a weapon strengthened my odds quite a bit.

"I'm gonna have to retie you, Charlie," he explained matter-of-factly, "but I'll let you sit up straight."

How kind.

The second my hand was free, I knew I had to make my move. I raked my nails across his face, then tipped the chair back and nailed him in the gut with my feet. It wasn't a strong hit but it took him by surprise, knocking him against the corner of the bed. He went over backward, landing hard on his neck, his legs in the air.

I didn't waste any time. I fumbled with my left hand to untie the cords around my right. Josh had the wind knocked out of him, but I knew he wasn't down for long. I felt like a pretzel twist, trying to reach across my body to work on the ropes while keeping my head raised to watch for Josh's next move.

He groaned, rolling to his side, his legs falling heavily to the floor. I scrambled to get the rope loose. I had a feeling he wouldn't get up in a good mood. My right hand and foot came free. As I directed both hands toward freeing the left foot I saw movement. Josh stood in front of me. Without thinking, I jabbed out with my right foot, catching him in the groin. Sorry, Josh, all's fair when defending your life.

He fell to the floor again, doubled in agony. I turned my attention again to my left leg and had it free in a few seconds. I scrambled to Josh's side, dragging the rope with me.

"Sorry about this," I said.

I wrapped the rope around his ankles, then pulled the end of it between his legs and bound his wrists. My knots were clumsy. I'd never pass the Girl Scout test now, but I hoped the rope would hold him awhile in his already weakened condition.

Pounding sounds from the front door brought me back to the bigger picture.

"Police! Open up!" they shouted.

"Come in!" I screamed.

The scene became a blur after that. Uniformed officers filled the house. Someone, thankfully, turned off the blaring television set. One man, the one who seemed in charge, congratulated me on subduing the suspect. I can't remember whether I acknowledged him or not.

I was sitting on the bed, examining my blistered wrists, when Kent Taylor walked in.

"We found the gun," he told me. "It was in his car."

"Was it the murder weapon?"

"We'll confirm that with ballistics tests, of course," he said, "but it's a nine millimeter."

"He admitted to me that he did them both," I told Taylor. "Of course, what he'll say in court is another thing. He also told me he'll get a good lawyer."

Kent shook his head in disgust. "Yeah, don't they all?"

He glanced around the room, taking in the cardboard boxes and folded bedding.

"What was going on here?" he asked.

"The child welfare people were making Josh move in with his aunt. I came over to help him pack. He kept telling me he wasn't going. Now, I guess he isn't."

"You want someone to take a look at those wrists?" he asked. "One of the men could drive you to the emergency room."

"Nah, that's okay. I'll doctor them myself when I get home." Suddenly, the idea of bundling up in my own quilt in my own bed was enormously appealing.

"I'll need a statement from you," Taylor said. At my expression, he added, "It can wait until tomorrow."

I shuffled through the house, making sure I hadn't left anything behind. I retrieved my purse from the kitchen and my jacket from the tatty recliner near the front door.

At home, I took a shower and put on my thick terry robe. I microwaved a cup of milk, added chocolate powder, and carried it to the living room. I smeared antibiotic ointment on my rope-burned wrists and wrapped them with a protective layer of gauze. I looked like an attempted suicide survivor.

It wasn't until I took the first sip of my hot chocolate that I realized I was a survivor. I could have very easily been Josh's next victim. My hands began to shake and I had to set the cup down. It was after one o'clock, but I knew I wouldn't sleep tonight.

At six o'clock Rusty woke me up by licking my fingers. In my exhaustion, I'd fallen asleep on the couch still bundled in my robe. My joints and muscles complained as I attempted to straighten them. I shuffled across the floor like a ninety-year-old to let Rusty out the kitchen door. I took two Ibuprofin and crawled into my own bed wearing only my wrist bandages.

The phone rang at eight, startling me out of the best sleep I'd had in ages.

"Charlie, it's Stacy." Her voice was breathy, excited. "Carla just called me. Is it true that you found the real killer?"

I mumbled that it was true, and suggested she meet me at the office in an hour. I closed my eyes, determined to get just ten more minutes. When the phone rang again forty-five minutes had passed.

Kent Taylor wanted to know what time I'd come down to give my statement. My heart jumped when I realized that I needed to be at the office in fifteen minutes. I told Kent I'd come downtown right after that. I pulled on clean jeans and a short sleeved cotton sweater and brushed my hair. The wrist bandages really stood out, so I swapped the sweater for one with long sleeves.

Stacy was waiting when I arrived at the office at five after nine. Her skin glowed again, her eyes sparkled.

"Have the police made it official yet?" I asked.

"Detective Taylor confirmed Carla's call right after I talked to you," she said. "Yes, it's official. Of course, now Brad's talking about filing suit for false arrest, but I'm just glad to have it over."

Of course. The *good* lawyer.

I filled her in briefly on last night's culmination of the search. I also informed her that I'd be sending a final bill for services. She didn't seem to mind.

"So, what now?" I asked.

She shuffled a little, knowing I was referring to her marital problems and the "deep" soul searching she'd done recently. Finally she said, "I don't know, Charlie. Brad's been very supportive these last few days. Maybe it will all work out anyway."

Yeah, maybe. How many years had she been telling herself that? I kept my mouth shut. She was a big girl. She'd decide for herself how much longer she could take his abuse. She left a few minutes later.

Kent Taylor was fairly accommodating, as police testimony goes. I gave my statement, most of which he'd already put together.

"There's one other thing I still haven't entirely resolved," I told him. "Who slashed my tire outside Penguin's Bar, and who followed me home last Friday night? I'm fairly sure I know who was behind it, but I'm not sure why." I told him about Tompkins and his big financial losses with Detweiller.

"Charles Tompkins is an investment banker, isn't he? He probably just wanted to hush it up about his own unwise money management. I'm sure it was nothing personal toward you." he said. "You can press charges on the tire slashing," he continued, shuffling the papers together inside the Detweiller file. "As for being followed home, you don't have any proof of that, do you? And no harm was done."

It was about what I expected from him. I told him not to worry about the tire. I left feeling a little down. I was poised to turn out of the downtown police station parking lot, when a thought hit me. I had to make one more visit to Larry Burke.

The red sports car was backing out of his driveway when I arrived. I sped ahead to cut him off, honking wildly.

"What the hell. . .?" Burke jumped from his car, ready for a fight.

"Just a couple of quick questions, Larry." I huffed the words out as I ran up the driveway.

"What questions? I thought you were done with this."

(BET THE FARM ?!)

"I'm just curious. Charles Tompkins had won big on a horse called Twist of Fate. Two days later Gary headed for Vegas, with you. Gary didn't skip out; he came back. But where's the money? Tompkins never got it."

Burke's perfectly capped teeth gleamed as he smiled. "This is rich, babe, I'll tell you."

I let the unwanted familiarity slide past.

"Old Gary did get greedy. He wanted to keep that money. Said Tompkins was a jerk who didn't need more than he already had. See, Gary had a real attitude about those people at that snooty country club. Couldn't believe they could have all the shit they had, and still want more."

"So he decided to keep a chunk of it for himself."

"Sure. Was Tompkins gonna make a big stink about it? And lose his reputation as an investment banker? Hell, a hundred grand sounds like a lot to you and me, but that guy takes home three times that much every year."

So, what meant more to him, a one-time jackpot or keeping the cushy job? I had a pretty good idea.

I filled in the blank. "So, Gary took the money to Vegas and the two of you blew it having the time of your lives."

He chuckled. "Actually, no. He had some other money, about five grand."

From the sale of Stacy's watch.

"We spent that. He took that whole hundred grand from the other deal and set up some kind of trust fund for his kid."

"What!"

"Yeah, had a lawyer do it up and all. I think the kid's supposed to get it when he turns twenty-one."

How ironic. A few more years and Josh would have been rich on his own. Now, I felt sure an investigation would take place into all Detweiller's business. As a convicted felon, Josh couldn't inherit, and if they dug deep enough they'd find out the money really belonged to Tompkins. His career would probably be ruined, but he'd get the hundred thousand. Of course, if Josh were never convicted...

Three days later I was sitting in my office, tying up loose ends. Stacy's final billing had gone out and I was now back on track with my tax returns, feeling better because I would get everything filed on time. I'd resolved not to worry about the outcome of Josh's trial. The little bit of press coverage I'd heard on the case only served to make me angry. It appeared that Josh had indeed gotten himself a good lawyer.

My travel agent sent my plane tickets and hotel confirmation for my vacation to Kauai. Six weeks away and believe me, I'm counting the days.